Cover design by Juan Villar Padron,
https://www.juanjpadron.com

Special thanks to my editor Janell Parque
http://janellparque.blogspot.com/

**To be the first to hear about new releases and
bargains—from Willow Rose—sign up below to be
on the VIP List.** (I promise not to share your email with
anyone else, and I won't clutter your inbox.)

- SIGN UP TO BE ON THE VIP LIST HERE :

http://readerlinks.com/l/415254

Tired of too many emails? Text the word:
"willowrose" to 31996 to sign up to Willow's VIP text List
to get a text alert with news about New Releases,
Giveaways, Bargains and Free books from Willow.

IT ENDS HERE

A REBEKKA FRANCK MYSTERY

WILLOW ROSE

BOOKS BY THE AUTHOR

MYSTERY/THRILLER/HORROR NOVELS

- In One Fell Swoop
- Umbrella Man
- Blackbird Fly
- To Hell in a Handbasket
- Edwina

7TH STREET CREW SERIES

- What Hurts the Most
- You Can Run
- You Can't Hide
- Careful Little Eyes

EMMA FROST SERIES

- Itsy Bitsy Spider
- Miss Dolly had a Dolly
- Run, Run as Fast as You Can
- Cross Your Heart and Hope to Die
- Peek-a-Boo I See You
- Tweedledum and Tweedledee
- Easy as One, Two, Three
- There's No Place like Home
- Slenderman
- Where the Wild Roses Grow
- Waltzing Mathilda
- Drip Drop Dead

JACK RYDER SERIES

- Hit the Road Jack
- Slip out the Back Jack
- The House that Jack Built
- Black Jack
- Girl Next Door
- Her Final Word

REBEKKA FRANCK SERIES

- One, Two…He is Coming for You
- Three, Four…Better Lock Your Door
- Five, Six…Grab your Crucifix
- Seven, Eight…Gonna Stay up Late
- Nine, Ten…Never Sleep Again
- Eleven, Twelve…Dig and Delve
- Thirteen, Fourteen…Little Boy Unseen
- Better Not Cry
- Ten Little Girls

HORROR SHORT-STORIES

- Mommy Dearest
- The Bird
- Better watch out
- Eenie, Meenie
- Rock-a-Bye Baby
- Nibble, Nibble, Crunch
- Humpty Dumpty
- Chain Letter

PARANORMAL SUSPENSE/ROMANCE NOVELS

- In Cold Blood
- The Surge
- Girl Divided

THE VAMPIRES OF SHADOW HILLS SERIES

- Flesh and Blood
- Blood and Fire
- Fire and Beauty
- Beauty and Beasts
- Beasts and Magic
- Magic and Witchcraft
- Witchcraft and War
- War and Order
- Order and Chaos
- Chaos and Courage

THE AFTERLIFE SERIES

- Beyond
- Serenity
- Endurance
- Courageous

THE WOLFBOY CHRONICLES

- A Gypsy Song
- I am WOLF

DAUGHTERS OF THE JAGUAR

- Savage
- Broken

1

It wasn't easy to tell whether the boy was dead or not. He was lying motionless on the wooden planks, his arms stretched out to the sides, and had someone entered the abandoned house on Second Street, they might have thought he was just sleeping, or maybe it was part of some game he was playing. There was no blood to indicate he had hurt himself or that someone had hurt him. There were no bruises and no wounds to indicate a crime had been committed or an accident had happened.

Outside, a thunderstorm approached, and lightning struck not far from the house, while buckets of water soon splashed on the boarded-up windows. Meanwhile, inside, there was a calmness unlike anywhere else in the world. There was just the boy, lying lifeless on the dusty floor that his mother would have told him—had she only been with him—was too dirty to be playing around on.

But his momma wasn't there. In fact, no one knew the boy was lying there, not breathing, arms spread out like Jesus on the cross.

No one would find him till many hours later.

2

"ALEXANDER? ALEX? WHERE ARE YOU, SON?"

Mrs. Cunningham walked out of the store and looked in the parking lot. Dark clouds were gathering in the distance, and she knew she didn't have long before the thunderstorm would hit them. A crack of thunder could already be heard in the distance, and the sky rumbled above her like an empty stomach. Her worried eyes scanned the area while she wondered where the boy could be. She had told him to wait in the car while she went to grab something at Webster Hardware and Farm Supply, and when she came out, the door to the car was open, but the boy wasn't there.

Could he have gotten out of the car? Was he playing somewhere nearby?

"Alex?"

Mrs. Cunningham walked around the car, then looked in the direction of the store across the street, called *El Curiosities*. Outside on display, they had the strangest water fountains and odd figures for your yard, including a colorful humanized rooster and a cow made of metal.

Alexander had been asking to go into that store ever since he heard that they had a real knight's armor in there. But he would have to cross the street to get to it. He wouldn't have done that, would he? He was only five. He knew he wasn't allowed to cross any streets.

She turned around and walked away, then looked at her watch. She had a charity event tonight and had to get home to get herself ready. Why did something like this always happen when you were in a rush?

She scanned the area around the supply store once again, looking for any movement or a red shirt poking out somewhere in the bushes behind it, but she couldn't see any. Then she sighed and decided he'd have to have gone to the store all by himself. The temptation might have been a little too big.

Mrs. Cunningham grumbled, then shut the car door and walked up to Market Boulevard, the main street going through town. Right before she crossed the street, she turned her head for a brief second and glanced toward NW Second Street behind the supply store, where she could see that awful abandoned house towering behind the trees, the one that no one dared to approach. Not just because of what had happened in there once, but also because they feared the roof might fall on someone's head one day. Why they hadn't torn the house down long ago was a mystery to most people.

"Alex?" she called as she approached the small store across the street. She approached the big figurines, then wondered who would possibly want a metal statue of a Mexican man playing guitar in their front yard. The fountains, at least some of them, she could understand, but those figures, it made no sense that anyone would buy them, except children.

Mrs. Cunningham scanned the front of the store, then called his name again, but received no answer.

A mother and her child were looking at the huge rooster.

"Have you seen a little boy? About this tall, wearing a red shirt?" Mrs. Cunningham asked, her voice quivering slightly.

The mother shook her head. "It's just us out here. Have you tried inside?"

Mrs. Cunningham shook her head, then stepped inside the store. There were rows and rows of useless junk everywhere, and she sighed as she walked down an aisle, then yelled her son's name again and again. At the end of the aisle, as she leaned against the wall, she found the armor, but there was no Alex there either. A salesperson in a green polo shirt, wearing a nametag reading Stu, walked by and she stopped him.

"Have you seen a little boy, five years old, wearing a red shirt? He might have come in here and looked at the armor. He loves anything about knights. You know how they are…boys at that age. If anything catches their interest, they'll stop at nothing to find it, not caring at all about rules and worried mothers."

The man shook his head. "No, ma'am. I haven't seen any children at all today, except for the little girl outside with her mother."

"Oh. Okay, thanks."

Disappointed, Mrs. Cunningham walked back through the store, then took it aisle by aisle once more just to be sure. When Alex wasn't there, she rushed back outside, where her eyes met that of the mother who had now moved on to look at a big reindeer with her daughter.

"Still haven't found him?" the mother asked while her

daughter giggled and touched the deer statue, petting it like it was a real animal.

"No. But if you do see him, tell him his mom is looking for him. I'll be right across the street in the parking lot in front of the supply store, where he was last seen. So, you can just call for me if you do see him, please."

"Of course. I will do my best to help," the mother said and sent her a sympathetic smile that in one way told her that she felt for her, but at the same time said *This would never happen to me. I always know where my child is.*

Mrs. Cunningham's eyes swept the area in front of the store once again before she crossed the road to get back to the car and see if Alexander had made it back yet. If he had, he was sure in for a scolding for leaving the car like that when his mother had told him to wait.

Maybe he went into the supply store to look for me, and I missed him somehow. Yes, that's it, she thought to herself. *He got bored in the car and wanted to know how much longer he had to wait.*

Happy that it was—of course—just a silly misunderstanding, Mrs. Cunningham went back into the store, and her eyes met the clerk's as she stepped through the door.

"Mrs. Cunningham, you're back already? Did you forget something?"

"Yes," she said, feeling silly for freaking out. "I seem to have forgotten my son. Is he here?"

Mrs. Cunningham locked eyes with the clerk for a few seconds, and she could tell he was searching for words. Her heart dropped when he shook his head.

"I am sorry, Mrs. Cunningham. I haven't seen him. Was he supposed to be in here? I didn't see him come in."

The blood left Mrs. Cunningham's face, and she rushed outside, now yelling her son's name in what could be mistaken for a scream, while panic settled in. She ran around the warehouse building housing the supply store, then back to the parking lot and looked down First Street, then back up at Market Boulevard. She ran up to the road and walked further down, yelling his name, then hurried back to the parking lot to see if he might have returned while she was gone, hoping and muttering little prayers under her breath.

He hadn't.

Frantically, she grabbed her phone from her purse and called her husband.

"I lost Alex," she said, barely getting the words across her lips. "What do you mean, *what do I mean?* I can't find him. He was in the car when I went into the supply store, and when I came back out, he was gone. What do you mean, *am I sure?* Do I not sound like I'm sure? Yes, I've searched everywhere. I'm telling you; he's not here. I'm scared. Where can he be?"

3
___

"I DON'T KNOW HOW YOU'LL DEAL WITH IT ALL ALONE," I said, holding the phone between my shoulder and ear. I reached a red light and stopped. "But you'll have to. There's no other way; I'm afraid."

"I can't believe you," Sune said, almost hissing at me. I hardly recognized him anymore. The way he spoke to me lately was so far from the way he used to adore me and everything I did. It was hard to tell that he had once loved me and I him. We had loved each other enough to have a child together. We had created a family, and now he had destroyed everything.

He was the one who had an affair with his nurse while in recovery from being shot. Once I found that out, I was done with him. I told him so numerous times when he asked me to forgive him and let him come back. It wasn't going to happen, I had said over and over. Now, Sune was with Kim, staying at her place and she had become a part of our lives. I didn't like her much—no that would be too mildly put—I loathed her. I couldn't even stand the thought of her. Yet I'd have to live with the fact that she was in my life, and—even worse—in my children's lives.

Sune had moved in with her in her condo not far from our house. I had stayed in the rented beach house and hoped I could afford to stay there until we figured everything out. But it required me making a lot of money, and that meant I had to work.

"Listen, I know you're busy with getting back to working again and spending time with your new girlfriend and all that, but you have to take your turn here. I've been taking care of all three kids for the past week, and now I'm asking for you to take them for three days. I know Julie is not your child, and therefore not your responsibility, but I also take care of Tobias when you need me to. We promised each other that we wouldn't separate the children, remember?"

"Of course, I do," Sune said, sounding less agitated. "I just don't think it's fair, Rebekka. You spring this on me the day before you leave and I'm just supposed to throw everything else I have in my hands and do as you tell me? What if I had a photo job?"

"Well, do you? Do you have a job?" I asked.

"No, not yet, but hopefully, I'll get some soon. I'm trying to get back to my life here, and that means I need to be available. Now, I won't be for the next three days."

I tried to control my anger. I could understand it if Sune actually had a job he needed to get to, but he didn't. I did, on the other hand. Why couldn't he just do this for me without complaining?

"I didn't get this assignment till yesterday," I said. "I know it's last minute, but I need to work; I need to eat too, Sune, and so do the kids. So, I have to take the jobs I can get. You're the one who wants us all to stay here in Florida so you can be with your precious nurse Kim. I don't mind it here; I actually love it here with the weather being so nice all the time and all, but when I discovered you with her, I asked for us all to go home. You didn't want that."

"I also asked you to forgive me and take me back," Sune said. "You wouldn't do that for me."

"No, I wouldn't because I can't trust you anymore and, frankly, I don't want to. But then when I asked if it wouldn't be for the best if we all went home, you said no. You wanted to stay so you could be with her. I agreed to stay, so William wouldn't lose his father, and the kids would still be able to be together, but that means I have to work as a freelancer and take whatever assignments I can get."

I paused to breathe when the light shifted, and I continued over the bridge onto the mainland.

"Don't you for one second think I like having to go do a promotional interview with some author about her next book, when I could be at home covering real stories for a real paper," I continued. "I could be writing about things that actually matter. Plus, I could be with my dad, who isn't doing too well. I'm doing all this for you, Sune. For you and the kids. So, you better help me out when I need it, okay?"

Sune was still silent and, for a second, I wondered if he had hung up. I heard him chuckle and rolled my eyes.

"You're with her, aren't you?" I asked. "You're not even listening to what I'm saying."

"So what if I am? Am I not allowed to hang out with my girlfriend?" he said, suddenly sounding like he was fifteen. Sune was the only man I knew who seemed to be maturing backward, getting more and more childish by the minute. It was ridiculous the way he acted these days, and I was sick of it, to be honest.

I exhaled, then accelerated. I hated the fact that my kids would be forced to spend time with her—the woman who had wrecked our home and caused us to split up—for the next couple of days while I was gone on the job. It was well-paid, so I could hardly have said no to it just because I didn't like Sune's new girlfriend. It was for *Metropolitan Magazine*, which wanted a feature on an author who lived inland and who had just published a book that had gone on to hit the *New York Times* bestselling list on the very first day. There were talks about a movie deal too. She was a very private person, and the magazine wanted me to do a story on her, trying to figure out who she really was. She had agreed to do an interview with me, but from talking to her on the phone, I got the feeling that she wasn't exactly excited about the idea.

"Just promise me you'll take good care of my children, will you?" I said, then hung up without waiting for his response. I felt tears in my eyes and a knot in my throat but swallowed it down along with my pride.

I hated what had happened to us.

4

WEBSTER, FLORIDA 1979

Carol watched the two girls sitting on the lawn and smiled while wiping her fingers on a dishtowel, removing flour and butter left on her hands from the peach pie she was baking for Anna Mae and her friend.

She liked to make things nice for Anna Mae when she came to visit her aunt. She wanted Anna Mae to like it at her house and hoped to be able to make up for all the bad stuff she had to witness at home.

It was no secret that Carol wasn't very fond of her sister, Joanna, or her choices in life, but she had the one thing that Carol couldn't get and that she desired more than anything in this world. A child. A beautiful angelic baby girl named Anna Mae.

Ever since she was born, Anna Mae had been the apple of Carol's eye. Her visits filled her with such profound joy that she always wished Anna Mae could stay a little longer. At one point, when her mother had been on yet another drinking bender, Anna Mae had stayed at Carol's house for five whole days, and that had felt like heaven for Carol. She had cherished the wondrous blessing of hearing a child's laughter in her home and often looked back on it as the best time of her adult life.

When Anna Mae wasn't there, the house felt so empty, so quiet. Then it was just her and John. Carol loved her husband, of course she did, but the fact that she hadn't been able to provide him with a child had come between them, and these days they barely touched or even spoke. Every time she looked into his eyes, she was reminded of her own failure, the failure of not being woman enough for him.

Anna Mae looked back at the house with her sparkling blue eyes, and Carol waved with a sigh. If only Anna Mae could have been hers.

Joanna doesn't deserve her.

It was the truth; she didn't. She didn't know how lucky she was and never knew how to appreciate her daughter. Not like Carol would. She would have spoiled that girl rotten had she only been hers. Instead, she was just her niece, and she'd have to be satisfied with only seeing her once in a while when her sister got tired of her or didn't want her around for some reason. More often than not, it was because she had men in the house or was drinking.

The oven dinged to let her know the pie was done and Carol pulled it out, closing her eyes briefly when the heavenly smell hit her nostrils. She put the warm peach pie on the patio outside to cool, then went over to Anna Mae and her friend, Bella, at the bottom of the yard.

As she approached the two girls, she took in a deep breath of the warm, moist air. Spring in Florida was always so wonderful, she believed. Summers were too hot and muggy for Carol, but spring was just perfect. Up above her, the sun shone from a clear blue sky, and there wasn't a sign of thunderstorms anywhere nearby. It was going to be a wonderful afternoon, well spent with her precious niece.

"Girls, the pie is ready," she chirped as she approached them. "Let's eat it while it's warm."

But the girls didn't react. They sat in the grass, heads bent down like they were doing something very important.

"Did you hear me, girls? Anna Mae? I said the pie is done. And I have vanilla ice cream to top it off with, just the way you like it."

Carol took a few steps closer to better see what they were up to, then gasped and clasped her mouth.

"Anna Mae! W-what…what are you…what are you doing to that poor bird?"

The girls both gazed up at her, their eyes beaming with wonder and amazement, while Carol stared at the bird in Anna Mae's hands. Anna Mae was holding it between her fingers while pressing down on its throat with her thumbs. The bird was flapping with one crooked wing and trying to get loose. It was obviously fighting for its life, while both of its legs had been snapped like twigs.

"Let go of that bird, Anna Mae," Carol said. "You can't hurt a poor bird like that. Can't you see that you're torturing it? Let it go, now."

The girl looked up at her, then pressed down her thumbs hard and choked the bird, holding it tight till it stopped moving. Then she smiled and sighed… almost like she was satisfied.

"Anna Mae," Carol said, shocked. She felt the hair rise on her neck despite the almost eighty degrees out. "What did you do? You killed it! Why would you do that to the poor birdie?"

Anna Mae finally let the bird drop from her hands, and her eyes followed it as it fell to the grass below.

"It's just a birdie," Bella said, lisping slightly.

Bella was a little slow, as they put it, so it didn't really shock Carol as much to see her engage in something like this, but Anna Mae should know better. She was the smart one of the two.

"It had a broken wing," Anna Mae said. "It couldn't fly anymore. So, it had to die."

"Did you break the wing?" Carol asked. "Did you, Anna Mae? Did you break its wing first?"

The girl didn't answer. She stared at the bird on the grass, and Carol wondered what to say to her next, how to talk some sense into her. It seemed almost like she didn't feel any type of remorse at all for killing that bird. It was obvious to Carol that Anna Mae had broken the wing first. How could such a young girl act so cruel?

Carol sighed, realizing she couldn't really scold Anna Mae since she wasn't her child. She didn't want to, either, since she didn't dare risk that the girl would never come back to visit again because she didn't like it at her aunt's place. Life without Anna Mae would be unbearable.

Carol sighed and straightened her apron.

"Now, get rid of that bird before we get rats or vultures crowding the place. You can bury it in the dirt over there and then come wash up. Like I said, it's time for pie."

5

MARGOT THREW HER HEAD BACKWARD IN LIGHT, ELEGANT laughter. A chilled glass of champagne lingered between her fingers, while subdued voices buzzed around her. People around her were making small talk, laughing in the same superior manner that Margot just had. For years, she had studied them, scrutinized their faces, and learned their every move. She knew in her sleep how the women held their glasses, how they carried themselves while sliding gracefully across the mahogany floors, how they let their heads fall backward in delight when the men said something amusing.

And she felt like one of them now. After years of trying to fit in, she finally felt at home among these people in their ten-thousand-dollar tulle gowns from Saks Fifth Avenue, their Mikimoto pearl necklaces, and Jimmy Choo or Manolo Blahnik high heels.

Theodore stood next to her, a cigar between his lips, a hand placed lightly on her back, like he needed to show the world that she belonged to him, and no one else.

Margot liked that feeling, and she liked being his. Never had she thought she'd experience love like this.

"How are you holding up?" he whispered as he leaned closer to her ear. "Are you surviving?"

"I think so," she said as their eyes met for a brief moment. "I'm doing a lot better."

Her stomach had been hurting before they left, but they both knew it was just nerves. Margot was never good at these charity events, but she went to them because it was expected of her. When married to the top neurosurgeon of one of the biggest hospitals in Florida, she knew she had to put on a brave face every now and then and make an appearance. So, she did it for his sake. She would do anything for Theodore. She loved him deeply and felt eternally grateful for how he had pulled her out of the poverty and misery she had once lived in. All that was gone, and she preferred it to stay that way.

"So, someone told me that you just published a new book?" a woman in a sparkling dress and very straight back asked her, smiling. "Isn't that exciting?"

Margot smiled and nodded shyly. She hadn't come to discuss her career. She was here for her husband and didn't want their attention.

She gave Theodore a brief look as if she was asking for his permission to talk about herself, and he nodded, his eyes beaming. He was proud of her accomplishments too, a fact that often filled her with reverential fear because where would she be without him? What if she lost him one day?

"Yes, you heard right. I did publish a new book recently," Margot said. "Only two days ago to be exact."

"And I hear it is doing very well," the woman continued. "Someone told me it was number one on the *New York Times* bestselling list? Isn't that marvelous?"

Margot blushed. She wasn't very fond of talking about herself. She preferred the blessing of living a quiet existence.

"Yes, it is, thank you. It has been truly amazing. I am very grateful for how well it has been received."

"I'll have to read it one day," the woman chirped. "I can't wait to tell people I know a real author, a *New York Times* bestselling one on top of it. Theodore must be so proud of you. You two make such a perfect and successful couple."

She smiled and winked at Margot, who once again felt the blood rush to her face. To think that anyone would brag about knowing her seemed incomprehensible.

"Thank you; you're being too kind. All I really did was to sit down and write a bunch of lies," she said.

That made the woman in front of her laugh. "Oh, that's a good one," she sang. "*I just sat down and wrote a bunch of lies.* Now, that one I'll have to remember when I tell all my friends that I know Margot Addington, the author."

Margot sent her an uncomfortable smile, then lifted her glass and poured the clear bubbles into her mouth, hoping they would calm her down. Margot had never felt pride over being who she was before this day, but right now at this moment, she did. For just a short, treacherous second, she glanced into one of the window-sized mirrors covering the walls of the ballroom and allowed herself to like what she saw.

6

―――――

"I put you in number fourteen. It's the first building to your right. You can't miss it once you get out there."

The small woman behind the counter looked at me over her glasses. Her nametag said, Adeline. Adeline smiled kindly and handed me the keycard.

"I'll find it. Thank you so much," I said, then rolled my suitcase back outside and turned right.

I had booked a room in a motel in downtown Webster, a small town that bragged to have exactly one thousand and ninety inhabitants on its sign just outside the city limits. It was a town that was known for its huge market, which they proudly called the world's largest, and for growing cucumbers. The motel was the closest—and cheapest—I could find close to where the author lived. It was only about a ten-minute drive away.

I slid the card into the lock and entered the small room, then threw myself on the bed, the springs creaking, almost screaming, underneath me.

I looked at my phone and saw that I had received a text from my daughter, Julie. She had recently started middle school, and that hadn't been without challenges. I had thought it would mean her growing more independent, but lately, it was like she needed me more than ever, like she was almost clinging onto me. I guessed it also had to do with what was going on between Sune and me, and I felt terrible for bringing her into the situation. Especially with everything else that had been going on in her life. She had been through a horrifying kidnapping ten months ago, where she and nine other girls were abducted in a school bus and buried underground in a moving van. Even though it had ended well for her, it still gave her nightmares, and it made it hard for her to be out in public. It took forever for me to get her to go back to school, and she refused ever to ride the bus again.

I MISS YOU, she wrote.

I glanced at the time. She was still at school but had to be on her lunch break. It was the only time they were allowed to use their phones during the school day, and she always texted me then. It broke my heart because it made me realize she probably didn't have anyone else to talk to. Julie hadn't wanted to hang with her friends much since the kidnapping. She had been clinging onto me instead, going wherever I went and never letting me out of her sight as soon as she was home from school. She often texted me several times a day, between classes, to make sure I was still close. I knew it was just a phase, and I was doing my best to embrace it, but it was wearing on me, especially since I felt terrible for her. I knew she was scared, and I couldn't make that go away.

I had signed her up for counseling right after she came back to me, and she had gone a few times but had finally ended up crying, telling me she didn't like talking to this counselor, that she didn't want to go back there. I had made her go a couple more times, then gave in and let her stop. I couldn't bear the crying when I took her there. Instead, I tried to talk to her about the event and how it had changed things for her. The counselor had given me some tools to help her along the way, and he believed she was going to be fine eventually. I felt like it made a big difference to her when I spent time with her, if I showed her that I cared about even the small things in her life and showed genuine interest in her and remembered to ask how she was feeling.

But it was tough. Boy, it was rough.

I MISS YOU TOO, I replied. HOW'S YOUR DAY GOING?

NOT GOOD, she wrote back. SOMEONE SPLASHED KETCHUP ON MY FACE AND SHIRT, AND NOW I SMELL.

I grumbled. Why did middle school have to be such a terrible place? Last week, someone had taken her lunchbox and thrown it across the lunchroom, so her food was completely squashed when she finally got it back, and she had no time to eat. It wasn't that she was being bullied; it was just people goofing around and making it harder for her to settle in. The kids there found it hard to respect her personal space, and there was always someone bothering her, taking her stuff, or just being annoying. It was usually the boys who did the stupid stuff, and I remembered from that age how awkward they were and how the girls were so mature that it made the boys even more insecure and goofy when around them. Plus, there were all the groups of popular girls looking down on everyone else while they fought for their positions among themselves. It was a terrible time for all involved, and Julie had never really found her position. At least not yet. On top of it all, she had gotten her period recently, and the hormones were running amok in her body, wreaking havoc, making her act out and become this creature I didn't know how to handle.

GO TO THE RESTROOM AND WASH IT OUT.

I'LL HAVE WET HAIR THEN. IT'LL LOOK GREASY. PEOPLE WILL THINK I DIDN'T SHOWER.

BETTER THAN SMELLING LIKE KETCHUP.

OK.

I grabbed my laptop and opened it, then found all the research I had done to prepare for the interview tomorrow. It wasn't exactly a complicated story, but I still liked to come prepared.

I MISS YOU, MOM, Julie wrote again. I'M IN THE BATHROOM CRYING.

I exhaled, feeling terrible. I was too far away to help her. There really wasn't anything I could do. It broke my heart, but she had to learn how to deal with these things herself. The girl was thirteen; she should be able to be away from her mother for three days, right?

Maybe if she hadn't been kidnapped and held captive for days underground. Maybe if she hadn't thought she'd never see her mother again.

I texted Sune and let him know what was going on. He wrote back that he had just gotten an assignment for some local paper, so he was out right now, but he would try and drop by later with a clean shirt for her and drop it off at the front office. I thanked him, then texted Julie to let her know.

IT'LL BE FINE. DON'T CRY ANYMORE, BABY.

I put the phone down and returned to my preparations, but I kept picturing Julie all alone in the restroom, not daring to leave because people would be able to tell she had been crying.

The counselor had told me I should be flattered that

Julie preferred to talk to me, that she came to me with every little emotion and trouble in her life because it meant we had a very strong bond. Believe me; I certainly was thrilled to be able to be there for her, and that I was the one she came to, but it felt like I was constantly putting out fires.

OKAY, she answered. I WASHED IT OUT. I'LL GO TO CIVICS NOW.

THAT'S MY GIRL.

SEE YOU LATER.

LOVE YOU.

And just like that, yet another fire had been extinguished. There would be a few hours before she would be able to text me again, so that meant I had time to prepare and read through the little I had been able to find about this mysterious author, Margot Addington.

7

"WE DON'T HAVE ENOUGH WOOD TO FINISH IT. WE NEED some more."

Peter looked down at his younger sister with a sigh. He had promised her he would build her a treehouse in their old magnolia tree in the backyard. It had been her dream for years to get a real treehouse, and since their dad was always out of town and never had time to do it, Peter had stepped up and said he would help her out.

So far, he had managed to build a platform, but then he had run out of wood. Until now, he had used the scraps his dad had lying in a pile in the back, but now there were no more.

"But…what do we do?" Rita, his sister, asked, her big green eyes lingering on him with great anticipation. "How do we get more wood? We need a lot because I want it to be a big treehouse."

Peter glanced toward their house. Their mother wasn't home since she was working down at City Hall and wouldn't be back until about two hours from now. Peter usually took care of his sister after school, and they weren't supposed to leave the house. Still, Peter had promised he would finish the treehouse today, and he never was one to break a promise to his younger sister, whom he adored so greatly. She could be a pain in the butt, yes, but he loved her dearly and would do anything to make her happy. Especially now that their parents had sprung the D-word on them and told them things were going to change and that their father would soon be living somewhere else. This was no time to make Rita sad about anything. If there ever was a time Peter felt like he owed her a treehouse, it was now.

"I think I might know a place where we can get some wood," he said. "But you can't tell Mom, you hear? You have to promise me that you won't say anything. You can't tell her where we got it from or that we left the house to get it. Do you understand?"

Rita looked up at him, then nodded in agreement. "I won't say a thing. My lips are sealed so tight that I can't even move them, see?"

"Good, then let's go, but we must hurry, so Mom doesn't know we've been gone," he said and grabbed his sister by the hand and dragged her out of the yard and into the street. They walked two blocks down and then stopped in front of a house.

Rita gulped when she realized where they were. "In there? Are you serious? Please, tell me you're kidding. This is where you want to find the wood? You want to go in there?"

He nodded. "There's tons of scrap wood inside of it. I've done it before, lots of times. The house has been abandoned for more than fifty years. No one cares about it or if we take the wood from inside of it. No one cares about the house at all. I bet no one even knows the wood is in there."

Rita stared at him. "But it's *that* house, Peter. You know

24

what happened, right? You know that someone died in there, right? And you want us to go inside?"

He shrugged. "So what if someone was once found dead in there forty years ago? People have died in a lot of houses. That doesn't mean the wood can't be used for building our treehouse. There's nothing wrong with that wood, and it's just sitting there, unused. Do you want the treehouse or not? Then, come on."

He pulled her by the hand, and they walked up the creaking stairs to the front door. Peter then pushed the door open, and they walked inside through a cloud of dust and dirt. Rita hesitated at the threshold, unsure if she dared go any further into the darkness of the house when her brother told her to hurry up.

"We don't have all day. If you want that treehouse to be finished, you better come quickly. We have to make it back before Mom gets home. Otherwise, we're going to be in so much trouble."

"We're gonna be in even more trouble if she finds out where we were," Rita mumbled and took the first step inside. "She's always told us to stay away from this place."

"Because of old superstition," he said. "I don't believe all that stuff. It's just an old empty house, that's all."

As her brother turned his head back and faced the darkness in front of him, he spotted something lying on the floor in the middle of the old living room. Rita saw it too and froze in place, sweat springing to her forehead.

"W-what's that? What's that over there, Peter? Peter?"

Peter bit his cheek while staring at the boy lying on the floor, flat on his back, arms stretched to the sides. The boy wasn't moving, and his chest wasn't heaving.

"P-Peter? I'm scared," his little sister said and tugged at his sleeve. "Can we please go back now? Please, Peter? I want to go home. I don't care about any stupid wood or the treehouse anymore. I just want to go home now."

Peter nodded and backed up, pulling his sister with him, his heart pounding in his chest.

"Me too, come on let's go," he said, then turned around and ran into the street, keeping his sister close to him.

Panting and agitated, he looked up the street and spotted two of the town's electricians who were working by a lamppost, then called out to them, waving his arms. When they heard what he had found, they rushed inside the house, Peter following them but staying with his sister in the doorway. One of the men gave the boy CPR while the other called for an ambulance. Peter watched the scene, his sister's hand clutched in his.

"Do you think he's dead?" she asked in a whisper like it wasn't polite to say out loud. "Do you think the boy is really dead, the way Grandpa was dead when we buried him?"

Peter stared at the man who was trying to breathe life into the young boy, yet the small body remained lifeless. Then, he nodded.

"I think so."

His sister shook her head.

"We never should have come here. Now we're going to get in all sorts of trouble once Momma finds out. She ain't gonna be happy about this one bit; that's for sure."

8

It was Mrs. Adeline's daughter, Regina, who stood behind the counter when I came in later in the day. She smiled when I asked where would be a good place to eat and recommended a place called Farmer's Market.

"I go there often with my mom," she said. "We've been going there since I was just a child. It's where most folks around here eat. They serve good old country style food."

"That sounds right up my alley," I said and smiled at the woman in front of me. She looked to be around my age and seemed pretty normal. I figured I could trust her recommendation. "I'll give it a try then and see if it's as good as you say."

I drove there in my car while looking around at the strange small town. The houses here were built in the old Florida style with wooden porches and screen doors. Many of them had overgrown yards and huge trees with Spanish moss hanging from their branches. I knew we were close to the Green Swamps and the landscape here was definitely a lot rougher and wilder than out by the beach where I was living. It was in places like this that they usually said there was a gator in every waterhole.

I shivered, thinking about my own run-in with a big gator about ten months earlier when trying to save Julie and her friends, and I felt my thigh where it had sunk in its teeth. I still had an ugly scar there that William thought was the coolest thing in the world. For me, it took some getting used to, especially when wearing a bikini.

I drove past the church and City Hall and saw a few faces stare at my car, then continued down into a neighborhood, then came back close to the motel and realized I had probably taken a wrong turn. I looked around and spotted several police cruisers from the county's Sheriff's office parked outside an old house that looked to be abandoned. An old rusty truck was parked in the yard next to it, completely overgrown with bushes and grass. I drove up close and put my car in park, then got out. An old lady with a small white dog was standing there, peeking in.

I walked closer, then caught the eye of an officer. I showed him my press card.

"What's going on here? Can you tell me anything?"

The deputy sniffled. "Two kids walked inside the house and found the body of a young boy, unfortunately. Must have snuck in and got himself hurt somehow. He could have fallen on his head, they assume. It looks like an accident, a truly terrible one, though."

"That is awful. Wow, what a tragedy. Has the family of the child been notified?"

He nodded. I could tell it affected him deeply, but he tried not to show it to me. "They're doing that as we speak. Wouldn't want to be in any of their shoes right now. Worst part of the job."

"I bet. I can't even imagine having to tell parents that

their child won't be coming home. It must be heartbreaking. Devastating."

"It sure is, ma'am. It sure is."

His eyes drifted away, and I could tell he had to go, so I smiled sympathetically and thanked him, then walked back toward my car. The old lady stopped me.

"What a horror," she said. "What happened in there."

"I know," I said. "It's tragic."

She gave me a questioning look. "I haven't seen you before. You ain't from around here, are you?"

I shook my head. "I'm just in town for a few days. I'm staying at the motel not far from here."

"Ah, you're staying at Adeline's place. Well, that explains why you don't know the story."

"Know what story?" I asked.

"It's not the first time they've found the body of a young boy inside that house," she said. "Cursed, is what it is."

I nodded and smiled. "Well, as tragic as that is that this isn't the first time this has happened, it is kind of dangerous to walk into an abandoned house and play. Cursed or not, the house ought to be demolished so it won't happen again."

THE FARMER'S Market was an old southern-style buffet. It was also where they auctioned off cattle at noon on Tuesdays, I was told. People came from all over the state to sell off their animals. Most of the cattle they were going to auction off the following day were already there, so there was constant noise coming from outside the building where I ate my fried chicken and cornbread. I was surrounded by mostly men—and some women—in their jeans, boots, and cowboy hats. I felt like I had landed in a time warp and had to admit I enjoyed it immensely, even though I couldn't really let go of the thought of that poor boy's parents whose world had just crashed. I would never forgive myself if anything ever happened to William. Barely had I finished the thought—or my food—before I received a text from Sune.

WILLIAM WANTS TO SAY GOODNIGHT.

I smiled, grabbed my phone, and walked outside. There was a row of rocking chairs on the porch, and I sat in one while holding my phone close to my ear, talking to my son, whom I was lucky enough to still have with me.

9

"They found someone. They found a boy!"

Anna Mae stood by the end of the driveway and yelled at Carol. Carol walked out on the porch. The girl stared at her, her eyes beaming and a smile spreading across her lips. She hadn't seen Anna Mae all week and had been wondering how the girl was doing all alone with her mother. It was all she could think about lately, actually for the past many years since Anna Mae was hospitalized four years ago and had to have her stomach pumped. She had swallowed an entire jar of her mother's sleeping pills. At first, they believed that she had tried to commit suicide, but knowing Anna Mae, Carol knew that wasn't the case. The girl wasn't suicidal at all. No, Carol knew her sister, and she also knew her sister had probably forced Anna Mae to swallow the pills, trying to get rid of her. It wasn't the first time something like that had happened. When Anna Mae was younger, her mother had made her swallow stuff on several occasions as punishment when she had been bad, and oftentimes she had ended up in the hospital because of it. Why her sister wouldn't just let Carol take Anna Mae in and take care of her since she so obviously didn't want her, she didn't understand. She had begged her to let her have her so many times, but Joanna enjoyed saying no, enjoyed seeing her sister suffer when worrying about the poor child.

"What are you talking about, sweetie? What do you mean they found a boy? What boy? Where?"

"They found a boy inside the old house, the one on Second Street. He's dead."

A furrow appeared between Carol's eyes. "I…what?"

"Come on, Aunt Carol. Come and see. Everyone is down there watching. Come and have a look."

Carol stared at her pretty niece with the angelic face and pageboy haircut. She wasn't sure she wanted to go. She wasn't sure she wanted Anna Mae to go down there and look at some dead boy either. It sounded awful.

"Come on, Aunt Carol. You must come with me down there. It's spectacular!"

Carol sighed, then closed the door to the house and followed the girl, who grabbed her hand in hers and dragged her down the street. It was hot and humid out, and after only a few feet of walking, she was already sweating.

A crowd had gathered at the old house, mostly kids. There were several police cars parked both in the driveway and on the street. A deputy from the Sheriff's office was keeping people back, shooing the kids away, telling them to go home.

Anna Mae pulled Carol close and pointed. "Look, there he is. Over there. They put him on a stretcher."

Carol watched as the boy was carried out to the ambulance and put inside, then felt a knot in her chest. She knew the boy. He was the Petersons' kid. Timothy was his name. He played baseball in the street with the other boys and would always nod and greet her politely. She had liked little Tim. He couldn't have been more than what, five years old? Carol shook her head. What a tragedy. What an awful, awful tragedy.

"W-what happened?" she asked. "Is he…?"

Anna Mae nodded. "Yes, he's dead. Like really dead."

"But…how did he die? What happened to him? Does anyone know what killed him?"

A woman standing not far from her turned her head and answered. "They said he fell and hurt himself. Must have been a freak accident. I always said they should have torn this house down many years ago or at least blocked it off so the kids couldn't run inside and get hurt."

"Oh, that's awful," Carol said and clasped her mouth. She looked at her niece next to her. This was no place for children. "We shouldn't be watching this. Come on, Anna Mae; we're going home now."

The girl looked at her like she had lost her mind. "I'm not going anywhere. I wanna watch. I wanna see the dead boy."

Carol shook her head. "We shouldn't. This isn't a show; this is a scene of tragedy, and the police are asking people to leave, so we should. Come on. I'll take you home to your mom."

Anna Mae pulled her hand out of her grasp. "All the other kids are watching; they're not leaving, so why do I have to? Why do I have to go home when they get to stay?"

"Because it's not appropriate. And they shouldn't be here either. You're just a child, Anna Mae. You're supposed to be out playing, not staring at some dead boy. Besides, we need to let the police do their work. Come. I have some ice cream in the freezer we can get before I take you home."

Anna Mae sighed, then looked at her friends in the crowd.

"All right."

10

Margot Addington lived on a big estate about six miles from Webster. She had told me she could see me at ten o'clock the next day and I drove there early to make sure I would arrive right on time. I was a few minutes early, so I parked the car on the side of the road for a few minutes, texting Julie who had broken down earlier that morning and called me because she had a big math test today and she couldn't find her folder. Luckily, I knew where it was and was able to tell her. Now, I texted her to make sure she was all right before the test. She started the day with theater in first period, and the teacher sometimes let them be on their phones. She texted me back that she had found the folder and that she was okay, though she was scared and nervous since she had gotten a C on her last test.

Julie's grades had taken a dip this past fall. It was only natural, I told her, going from elementary school to middle school. Everything was different…the routines, the classes, the teachers, and it took some getting used to. On top of that, she had to remember what she had been through and give herself a break. It was okay to accept a bad grade every now and then, and it was okay not to feel okay all the time. Processing what she had been through took time.

Every now and then, Julie became an emotional wreck, and it made me feel so helpless. The counselor had told me it was very natural and to just let her have these episodes; she would always come back to me afterward. This was how she would learn to cope with her emotions. But it was tough seeing my girl struggle to deal with what went on inside of her.

I had never been an overachiever myself in school, but Julie was different than me. She always got straight As and getting a C on a test crushed her self-esteem. She was ambitious, and I saw that as a good thing, but I feared for her mental situation if she kept pressuring herself the way she did. I didn't want her to become one of those perfect girls who thought all their worth was in getting straight As. Julie was so much more. She had saved the lives of several other girls last summer, and she was a lot stronger than she gave herself credit for. I saw greatness in her, but I wanted her to see it too.

As time passed and it was finally ten o'clock, I drove up to the gate, then pressed the button on the intercom, and a voice answered. The gate soon opened, and I drove onto the estate.

I had barely gotten inside before I realized they had horses. I had always loved horses, and Julie used to do a lot of horseback riding before we came to Florida. I had been meaning to find a place for her to start up again, thinking it would be good therapy for her.

The main house was a large building looking almost like one of those mansions taken out of some old '80s TV show like *Dallas* or *Dynasty*. It was huge. I parked and got out, grabbed my computer bag, then walked up to the front door.

An elegant woman wearing jeans, a soft silky shirt, and a scarf wrapped loosely around her neck, greeted me. She had long blonde hair and seemed almost perfect in a way that made me slightly uncomfortable. She was nicely dressed, but not overdressed. She wore make-up but not so much it was visible.

She was a woman who knew how to play her part.

"You must be Rebekka Franck," she said and held out her hand.

Her beauty startled me slightly, and I felt out of place, awkward even. I reached out my hand and shook hers, almost dropping the bag in my hand.

"Yes, and you must be Margot Addington?"

She nodded and smiled. "That I cannot run from. Let's go inside; shall we?"

11

————

"You're a very private person," I said after taking another sip of my coffee and putting the cup down. "I could hardly find any information about you online."

We were sitting in Margot's office, and she had shown me where she worked. Her desk was placed by the window, with the most gorgeous view over a lake and the horses next to it. The room was covered with bookshelves from top to bottom. There was a calmness and quietness to it that I really enjoyed.

"It's very rare these days with the growing competition for readers' attention. Today, most authors have a solid social media presence with many followers that they engage with daily. They do interviews for magazines and book signings that they remember to tell about on their blogs and Facebook. It's a big part of their marketing strategy, to be reachable, but not you. I take it you've never done any interviews before?"

"Writing books for me was never about obtaining fame or even making money. I write them because I love to write. I don't think the world really cares much what I think about politics or the environment. I can hardly imagine why they would care about who I am. My persona isn't important for my stories, I believe. I like to let the books speak for themselves," she said, her eyes avoiding mine for a brief moment. "The person behind the books isn't that interesting. The stories I write are. I always hoped that would be enough."

I wrote a couple of notes on my pad, then looked at a framed picture on her desk. The picture in it was of her with a young girl.

"Nevertheless, I know that many readers are dying to know more about you," I said. "The most I could find were speculations about you and who you were. So, let's tell them a little about you; shall we? Let's start with your family. The girl in the picture, is that your daughter?"

Margot looked at the frame, then grabbed it and held it between her hands. "Yes, this is Minna. It's short for Vilhelmina. She's the best thing that ever happened to me," Margot said, not taking her eyes off the picture. "But please don't put her name in your article."

I shook my head. "I don't have to. I'll just mention that you have a daughter. It'll make you more human to a lot of people. You'll be relatable, and that's what we're going for, right? Now, what is Minna like? Does she have any interest in writing like her mother?" I asked.

"No, none whatsoever. I guess she takes more after her father. Science is her thing," Margot said and put the picture back. "She won the state science fair three years in a row, and she wants to become a doctor like her dad."

"And your husband, Theodore Addington, is a neuro-surgeon, right?" I said. "Him, I could look up easily. He's been quite successful?"

"Yes. He's currently at Leesburg Regional Medical

Center. He was headhunted for this position a couple of years ago, so we moved here from New York."

"And I take it he has been able to provide for you while you focused on your writing? That must have been quite amazing for you, " I said, feeling a little sting of jealousy. I had always wanted to write novels, but since I became a single mom, I had to work to take care of Julie and myself. Not that I minded, I liked working as a reporter, but every now and then it would be nice to be able to sit down and make up your own story and not have to constantly go searching for it. I couldn't help thinking Margot Addington had something great going here.

"Yes, that worked out quite well for both of us. I actually started writing when Minna was a newborn, and I was at home a lot taking care of her. I would write when she napped or later on when she was away at pre-school. A couple of hours here and there soon led to my first book, and later, more followed. People often ask me how I manage to write a book, and usually, I tell them that if you just write one page a day, then after a year you'll have an entire book. Now that Minna is older, I have a lot more time to write, though, and can do it full time."

"And how old is Minna now?" I asked.

"She just turned eleven."

"My daughter is thirteen," I said. "So, they're close in age."

Margot wrinkled her nose. "It gets worse, doesn't it? I feel like she's already a full-blown teenager, but I have a feeling it's only the tip of the iceberg; am I right? There's more to come?"

I exhaled, thinking about Julie and how things had gotten so different over the past six months. It had been nothing like what I pictured it would be to have a teenager. I had imagined something different like her slamming the doors and yelling at me, and her rolling her eyes at me, but that wasn't how she was. She was just so needy all the time. It was almost like she found it hard to deal with even little things in life, things she never worried about before.

"It's…different," I said. "Some days are really great, but then others…"

"You don't know what hit you, right?"

"Something like that." I looked at my notepad, trying to get the conversation back to be about her, the author, the person Margot Addington. I felt like she kept turning the conversation away from herself.

"So, you write mysteries, but they all have a touch of horror to them. I read your latest book, *The Terrible Death of Angus McMannus*, and thought it was quite gory for a mystery. Where do you get that dark side from?"

Margot strained a smile, then shrugged. "I really don't know, to be honest. I am a fairly decent person, who doesn't even like to watch horror movies, and I can't stand to see blood. But it's different once I sit down at the computer and start tapping. It just comes to me, and then I write it down."

"So, you don't plan for them to be gory or even brutal? Because I have to admit, they are quite ruthless. To me, it's surprising that such a beautiful and together woman like you can write something like that. How do you get your ideas?" I asked.

"I usually get my ideas when going horseback riding or on my walks around the lake. I can't tell you how or where it comes from; it just does. It just sort of pops into my mind. It always begins with a question, *What if?* And then my imagination takes it the rest of the way."

I nodded, remembering having read other authors say something similar. It was just a little strange to me that you could be this normal person, a very elegant and delicate lady living in beautiful surroundings, and then you write about these horrifying events in such deep detail it had made me shiver and become a little sick to my stomach, to be honest.

But that was probably why she was the author, and I wasn't.

12

MARGOT STOOD BY THE WINDOW IN HER LIVING ROOM. SHE watched the woman as she got back into her car, while peeling an apple with a small kitchen knife. The journalist-woman put her computer bag in the back, then slammed the door shut and went to the front.

Margot sighed, then kept peeling the apple without looking at it. Soon, she had created a long winding peel that spiraled toward the floor.

Theodore came up behind her. She didn't hear him until he spoke, and it startled her. Her finger slipped, and the blade came too close to her skin. It was bleeding, and Margot stared at the blood.

"How did it go?" he asked. He stood close to her, and she could feel his warm breath on her ear. "How was the interview? Did you survive?"

Margot looked at the blood on her finger and turned it in the light. A drop dangled from it for a few seconds before it let go and fell into the abyss. It died on the tiles below. Margot stared at the small splatter of blood beneath her while the car's engine started outside in the driveway. Margot put the finger on her lips and sucked the blood away.

"I think it went okay," she said. "It wasn't too bad. The woman they sent was very nice and didn't seem like she wanted to dig up dirt, but you never know. She might write some anyway; you know how they are. They'll just make stuff up if they can't find any."

Theodore placed both his hands on her shoulders and squeezed. "I'm glad it went well, and I'm glad you did it. The publishing house has been trying for years to get you to do some interviews, and I, for one, I think it's about time. I know you like to remain private, but it's time you show the world who you are. Plus, it will help spike sales. Selling books isn't as easy as it used to be. Things are changing in that industry. Those who connect with their readers will be the winners. You can't hide forever."

Margot stared into the driveway as the journalist drove off, then shuddered slightly. She thought about the talk she'd had with her agent, Edward, a few days earlier. He hadn't ordered her to do the interview, but it was close. No wasn't an answer he was going to accept this time.

"Your publisher will toss you, Margot," he had argued when she said she wasn't going to do it, "for some young and more exciting writer who has thousands of followers on social media. They expect you to be out there now, to be visible. People demand to know who Margot Addington really is. Who is the person behind the name and those nail-biting books? I'm not asking you to make a YouTube channel and broadcast daily from your everyday life. It's not like that. I'm only asking you to open up a little bit. You have to give them something. And, to be honest, it isn't much they're asking. It's just an interview, Margot. It doesn't even have to be a long and deep one. Just tell them about your day and where you get your ideas from, how your daily routine is. Stuff like that."

After hanging up with her agent, Margot had considered stopping writing altogether. She wasn't sure it was worth it if this was how it was going to be.

"You'll be happy you did it," Theodore now said, still squeezing her shoulders. "Just wait and see once the article comes out. You'll probably want to do many more once you get the taste for it. Fame is like a drug."

Margot cut a piece of the apple and bit into it. The car was at the end of the dirt road now. For a brief second, she wished another car would ram into it as soon as it left the estate.

"I know it was unpleasant to talk about yourself, but at the end of the day, you'll be happy that you did it," he added. "I know you will."

Margot chewed the juicy bite of apple while going through the interview in her mind. Had she told her anything that the journalist could twist in any way to make her seem unpleasant? Had she revealed too much about herself? Would the reporter make her sound like an idiot?

"The photographer will be here tomorrow to take your picture for the article. After that, it'll be all over," he said. "I'll make sure to buy the magazine when it's published and frame it for you. I'll hang it on the wall in your office."

Margot sighed and finished the apple. Theodore turned her around and looked into her eyes.

"This is good for you, Margot. It was a great opportunity; one that you'll be glad you didn't turn down. *Metropolitan* is a big magazine, and it's national. It'll do wonders for your career."

"Then why do I feel like I've made the biggest mistake

of my life?" she asked. "Why do I feel like I've just ruined everything?"

That made Theodore laugh out loud. "Oh, you silly woman. It was just one interview. I don't see how that can ruin anything. What could possibly go wrong?"

13

Carol was sitting in her kitchen, reading, when the front door opened. She looked up, wondering who it was since she wasn't expecting anyone. John was at the auto shop all day.

"Hello?" she said and rose to her feet. "Is anyone there?"

There was no answer. The door was still open with the screen door clapping against the doorframe in the wind.

"John? Is that you?"

Still, no one spoke. Carol walked out of the kitchen and toward the front door. She closed it, wondering if it could have been the wind. As she turned, her heart skipped a beat. In the hallway, under the big chandelier, stood Anna Mae. She looked up at her from behind her bangs, her angelic blue eyes smiling eerily.

Carol clasped her chest. "Boy, you scared me, Anna Mae. What are you doing here?"

"I came from school," the girl said. She held out a piece of paper toward Carol. "I made a drawing. It's for you."

Carol realized that Joanna had asked Anna Mae to go be with her aunt today, probably because she had men visiting as usual. Carol shuddered at the thought.

Anna Mae had told her stories about what went on in her home, and Carol had once confronted her sister about it, but only received the answer that she didn't have to take care of Anna Mae if she didn't like it. She had said that to shut Carol up since Joanna knew that Carol's biggest fear was that Joanna would take the girl away from her. But Carol had added one more thing. She had told Joanna to at least make sure the girl was out of the house when she had those men over. So now and then, Joanna sent Anna Mae to Carol's house whenever it happened.

"You made me a drawing?" Carol said happily. "I can't believe you did that. That is so sweet of you."

Anna Mae smiled. She held the drawing out toward her. "Here you go."

"I'll hang it up on the fridge, so I can look at it every day," Carol said cheerfully. So often, she had dreamt of having a daughter and hanging her artwork up on the fridge. It was a silly little thing, but for some reason, it was one of her biggest wishes.

Carol grabbed the paper and looked at the drawing, her eyes filling. Then her heart dropped.

"What is this?"

"My drawing," she said.

"But...but..." Carol looked at Anna Mae. "What is it? What's in the drawing?"

"It's the boy," Anna Mae said. "I made a drawing of the boy in the house for you. I gave it a title. It's called *the boy who died*."

"So...let me get this straight," Carol said, her hands getting clammy. "It's a drawing of the boy who was hurt in the old abandoned house. You drew him… when he was dead? How do you know…what it looked like?"

Carol stared at the picture. She had read in the paper how the boy was found, how he laid on the floor, arms spread out, looking like Jesus on the cross. But how did Anna Mae know this? How did she know it in enough detail to draw it?

"I was there," Anna Mae said. "I saw him in the house, remember? I saw him lying there with his arms out like that."

Carol stared at the young girl, then she smiled, relieved. "You're talking about afterward. You were there after he was found and when the police were there too. Of course, I remember that. And since everyone is talking about this, it's only natural for a child to make a drawing of it. Of course, it is. It's not odd at all. It has been on everyone's lips. It must have been quite traumatic for all you kids around here. Of course, you would draw it. Say, have you had any lunch?"

The girl shook her head, but Carol already knew she wouldn't have. Joanna never made lunch for the girl, and she was usually starving once she came to Carol's house.

Carol grabbed Anna Mae's hand in hers, and they walked to the kitchen. Carol hung the picture up on the fridge, then made peanut butter and jelly sandwiches for them both. She couldn't help staring at the drawing while they ate together. It wasn't exactly what she had pictured her first drawing on her fridge to look like, but it was what she got. And if there was one thing life had taught her, it was to work with whatever God gave you in life.

14

I STARED AT MY SCREEN. THE LAPTOP HUMMED, dissatisfied, on the desk in the hotel room. I had been staring at it for hours now, not knowing my angle on this article.

Margot Addington had given me nothing to work with. She had barely told me anything useful. Not even when I asked about where she got her ideas did she open up to me. That was usually the one authors loved to talk about. That was the easy question, the icebreaker.

But her answer had been that she didn't know. How was I supposed to write an article out of that?

I tapped on the keyboard, trying to get at least something on paper, but as soon as I had written the first two sentences, I deleted them again. This would never make it into *Metropolitan Magazine*. I grumbled angrily. I had to do well on this story if I wanted my career to take off as a freelance writer over here. It was the only way to be noticed and get other assignments. I wanted to get this going, and I wanted to get to a point where they'd trust me with real stories, the important ones like I had been used to back home. They didn't know me here; they didn't know how good I was. And the way this interview had gone, I wasn't sure they ever would.

I sighed and leaned back in my chair. The small motel room had a musty smell to it. The carpet was a color I wouldn't even know how to categorize. Was it orange? Was it red? I wasn't sure.

Stop procrastinating; will you?

I stared at my notes and then played the recording of my interview again. There were a lot of *I don't knows,* and *I don't remember much about that* for answers. There really wasn't anything worth basing a story upon. Could one person really be that uninteresting?

I had been extremely jealous of this woman as I saw the place she lived and the life she lived, being able to make a living from her beautiful home and being so successful at it. But I was disappointed at how terrible the interview had gone. I had thought this woman would have so many interesting things to tell the world. I had tried and tried, fishing for something, but it hadn't come. Instead, I had to almost pull the answers out of her. I couldn't believe it. Could someone who wrote these gory and very thrilling mysteries really be that boring?

"Maybe that's your story," I said into the room. "Maybe you should just write about how dull this woman really is."

As if it had heard me, my phone buzzed on the desk. Fearing it was my editor asking for the story already, I glanced at the display. To my relief, it was Julie. She had probably come home from school and wanted to chat.

I picked it up.

"Hi, baby. How was your day?"

"It was okay. At least better than yesterday," she said.

"So, no ketchup incidents, I take it?"

"No. Today was good. No accidents or anything."

"That's great, honey," I said, feeling relieved. I was learning to cherish the days when she was happy. "I'm glad you had a good day."

"How about you?" she asked. "How did the interview go with that author?"

I sighed and glanced at the blank page. "Eh. The interview wasn't too great, to be honest with you. Now, I'm just trying to get this story down on paper so I can come home. I can't wait to get back."

"How much time do you have to write it? When is your deadline?" she asked.

"They need to have it tomorrow morning," I said, feeling the stress nagging in my stomach. "The editor wants to see it first thing when she gets in. Then we can do edits later tomorrow, but they need the first draft by then. But talking about it stresses me out, so let's talk about something else. How are the others? How are Tobias and William?"

Julie took a second to answer. "They're fine. Tobias is on his computer, and William is going in the pool."

"How's Sune doing?" I asked. "Did he remember to make your lunches this morning?"

"He did. They were actually pretty good. He made a pasta dish for me and some fruit in a small container. I also got a small piece of chocolate for dessert."

"That sounds great," I said, feeling impressed. "Maybe we should have him make all our lunches from now on, huh?"

"But she's here too, Mom," Julie said. "She's here all the time now."

"Kim?" I said. I felt a shiver run down my spine when thinking about the woman who had ruined everything, the woman who had stolen Sune from me. They'd had an affair while he was in recovery after being shot, and she was his nurse. I had been taking care of him, taking care of the kids and everything else, being the only one making money, while they were just sharing secret kisses at the clinic. It still enraged me when thinking about it. I was done with Sune, but it was hard to be completely separate when you had built a family together. Thinking of her being with my children, with my boyfriend, made me want to scream. I was so angry with Sune for throwing everything we had out like that. How could he do that to us? How could he do it to the children? I knew things hadn't been easy lately; it hadn't been easy for any of us, and, no, I probably hadn't been as attentive to him as he needed me to be, especially not physically. But he was the one who had pushed me away, not the other way around. And now he had found someone else.

"Yes, and she's cooking dinner. Some Asian dish, Thai, I think it is. With chicken. It smells awful. I don't think I can eat any of it."

I sighed. Julie had recently become a vegan, and that didn't exactly make any of our lives easier. I had hoped it was just a phase, but so far, it had lasted for two entire months. She refused to eat anything that wasn't plant-based. At first, I had indulged myself in cooking for her, trying out all these new recipes and found it to be quite fun, but as time passed, it was becoming a nuisance. It was simply too demanding.

"Then you'll just have to cook something for yourself," I said. "Listen, Julie, I need to write this article. Can we talk later?"

There was a pause.

"Oh, okay."

"I'm sorry, sweetie. It's just…I really need to write this thing. I'll call you before bedtime, okay?"

Another pause.

"Okay."

I hung up, feeling guilty. I could tell that Julie wanted to talk longer, but I didn't have the time for that. Not tonight. This article had to be in my editor's inbox first thing in the morning. If I didn't start writing now, I'd have to stay up all night and finish it.

15

It was past midnight before I finished it. I stared at the screen, wondering if my editor would be pleased. I had a feeling she wouldn't. She had probably expected something a little more exciting, but this was what she would get. It was all I had…all the woman would give me.

I realized I hadn't had anything to eat, so I left the room and got into my car. Nothing was open at this hour except for the Circle-K right outside of town. I drove down there and bought myself a hotdog and a polar-pop. A raccoon stared at me from behind the car as I walked back out. Its glistening eyes reminded me of our neighbor's dog that William was so fond of. Sune and I had always thought that dog looked like a raccoon. I took a picture of it with my phone and was about to send it to Sune when I remembered he was no longer my boyfriend.

I stared at the screen, then shook my head, feeling my eyes grow moist. I shook it off. It was no use feeling sorry for myself.

The raccoon ran off, and I got back into my car, then

drove back. A dead skunk was lying on the side of the road as I drove back onto Market Boulevard. It was bloated from the heat.

I drove down Second Street and then passed the abandoned house. It was still blocked off with police tape, but all the techs had gone home. Their work there was done. In the newspaper, I had read that it was an accident. The boy had played in there, then fallen. It was tragic, but nothing but an accident, the local Sheriff Travers was quoted saying.

I rolled past the old house slowly, unable to take my eyes off it. The entire yard was overgrown. A huge tree in the backyard had branches that looked like they reached for me. Ms. Adeline from my motel had told me they used to hang slaves from that tree, back over a hundred years ago when there had been a riot. It was said that the slaves still haunted the place.

I stopped the car in front of the old house and ate the rest of my hot dog while staring at it behind the yellow police tape. I had seen the boy's picture in the paper, and I kept imagining him walking in there. Why did he do that? What had drawn him to this place? Just curiosity? Probably.

I was about to start the car up again when I saw something that made me pause. I looked closer. If I wasn't much mistaken, then someone had come out of the back of the house, then took off running across the yard. I watched as this person reached the end of the property, and then disappeared over the fence.

I kept staring, not quite able to figure out if I had actually seen this person or if it was just the Spanish moss dangling from the big tree that had been playing tricks on me.

I decided to go look for myself. I jumped out of the car, then walked up to the old house. I snuck under the police tape and opened the creaking door. I walked inside into the darkness, using my phone to light my way. Two rats ran away from my light in the corner. Leaves were blown around as I opened the door and dust whirled into the air. I was careful not to touch anything as I walked into the living room of the old house. It was obvious there had been a lot of people there recently. I remembered the article I had read about the boy. He was the son of the local Cucumber King, one of the big shots in the community. He had lain in the middle of the floor, arms stretched to the sides, shaping a cross. I looked around me, wondering how he had managed to get himself killed. There wasn't really anything near where he was found that he could have crawled up onto and fallen. There were piles of wooden planks that had been broken apart from the floors, but those were at the end of the room, far from where the boy was found. There was half of a tree that had crashed into the side of the house, and the branches were reaching through the ceiling. Had he climbed a branch and then fallen? I asked myself, then kneeled. It didn't seem possible for him to kill himself by falling from there. A broken arm, maybe, or a leg. But death? It wasn't that great of a fall. There were toddlers who fell from skyscrapers and survived. The article hadn't said anything about what the cause of death was. Had he hurt his head? If so, there'd have to at least be blood, right? There didn't seem to be any blood anywhere.

It puzzled me.

I stared at the floor, searching for any signs of an accident when suddenly my light fell on something on the wall in front of me. Someone had written something on it.

I kill so that I may be eternal.

I shook my head, not remembering reading about any writing on the wall in any of the articles. I reached out and touched the last letter. My finger came back with red paint on it.

It was still fresh.

16

I STAYED UNTIL THE SHERIFF ARRIVED. I HAD CALLED THE station, but the deputy insisted they wake up the sheriff for this. Half an hour later, Sheriff Travers drove up slowly in front of the house and parked.

He got out of the car with much trouble, grunted and pulled up his pants, then staggered toward me. I had read in this morning's paper that Sheriff Travers was the long-time champion of the local pie-eating contest and that he was the man to beat again this year. It was obvious he trained for it all year round.

Sheriff Travers came up toward me, grumbling. "This better be good if you're dragging me out of bed. You the one who called it in?"

I nodded. "The name is Rebekka Franck. I'm a reporter."

Sheriff Travers lifted his eyebrows. "Reporter, huh? What are you snooping around here for? Didn't you see the *Do Not Cross* tape?"

"I wasn't snooping around. I saw someone run out the

back of the house while driving by. I went inside to check it out, and that's when I found it."

The sheriff stared at me, both eyebrows lifted. "That's called snooping where I come from, lady. Now, show me what you found. Some type of writing, you say?"

I nodded and walked ahead of the sheriff inside. I held the door for him, and he came in too. Still panting from the steps, he used his flashlight to shine on the wall. The letters had been running, and some of the paint had dripped onto the floor.

"Well, I'll be…" he said.

"I take it that wasn't there earlier. The paint is still wet."

"I see that," he said and approached it. He looked at it from top to bottom, then touched it with his finger. "Yup. Still as wet as a drowned rat."

Sheriff Travers pulled up his pants once again with a deep exhale.

"So, what do you make of it, Sheriff?" I asked.

He shook his head while letting his flashlight run over the letters once again. Then he sniffled.

"Nothin' but kids being kids," he said. "Childish pranks. I'll have someone wash it down in the morning."

With a grunt, he turned around.

"Are you sure about that?" I asked. "It seems like quite a disturbing prank. A little too much for kids, don't you think? I mean, what kind of a child would do that? Who would say that Alexander Cunningham was killed and didn't die accidentally?"

"Kids 'round here don't have much to do," Sheriff Travers said with a sly smile. "What ya gonna do, right?"

We left the house, and he closed the door behind him, putting a crime scene sticker on the door.

"There. That will hopefully keep the kids out of this place. I don't want anyone else to get hurt."

A sticker on the door? I was about to scream. How was a sticker supposed to keep the children out? If anything, it only filled them with more curiosity. Didn't the sheriff know anything about children?

He lifted his hat politely. "Now, if you'll excuse me, ma'am. It's gettin' late. I'd like to head back to my bed now. I imagine you'd like to see yours too. Good night."

I walked back to my car, feeling a little lost. I couldn't escape the thought that something was going on here that ran a little deeper than just children's pranks. Yet there was no way this sheriff would ever see that. And if he refused to, then who would?

17

Margot sat in her living room. The clock next to her blinked three a.m. She was sweating and couldn't find rest. A tightness in her chest refused to let go, and she could hardly breathe.

The light flickered on, and her husband stood in front of her in his jammies. He looked concerned.

"Margot? What are you doing down here in the middle of the night? Are you okay? You don't look well. Are you sick?"

Her hands were shaking. She hid them and forced a smile. "I'm okay. I just couldn't sleep. I have so much on my mind lately; that's all. I'll be up again soon."

He approached her, then knelt in front of her, taking her hands in his. As he did, he realized how badly they were shaking.

"You're trembling. What's going on, Margot?" he asked. His kind blue eyes looked up at her, scrutinizing her. "You haven't been yourself lately. Is it that silly interview? Is that what's been messing with your head?"

She forced a smile. "Maybe. You know how I don't like

these types of things. I get anxious. Now, I'm nervous about the article coming out and what they'll write about me. I don't like it, Theodore."

He smiled understandingly. "Foolish me. I shouldn't have pushed this when I know about your anxieties. I promise I'll never do it again, my love. I'll call Edward tomorrow and let him know this is the end of it. No more interviews. Now, it's time for the great Margot Addington to write and not do publicity. If the publishing house doesn't think that's enough, then so be it."

A tear escaped her eye and rolled across Margot's cheek. He wiped it away using his thumb.

"Don't cry, honey. You know you suffer from Social Anxiety Disorder. It's perfectly normal the way you feel right now. The heavy sweating, the difficulty breathing, it's all part of it. As your doctor, I should have known this. It's over now. You won't have to do any more interviews."

"Thanks, honey," she whispered with an exhale.

He rose to his feet and stretched out his hand. "Are you coming back to bed? You know how your anxieties get worse if you don't get a proper night's sleep."

As she took his hand and let him pull her up from the chair, he glared at her shoes. "Say, how did you get so dirty? Have you been outside?"

Margot felt her chest grow tight again, then looked away, nodding. "I wasn't feeling well, so I went to see the horses. You know how being with them always calms me down."

He stared at her, then down at her muddy shoes again. He lifted his gaze and smiled as he saw the jacket she was wearing on top of her nightgown. "Maybe you should leave the jacket and shoes down here."

She chuckled. "Of course."

Once she had taken both off, she walked up the stairs,

holding his hand in hers. They snuck past Minna's door, and Margot peeked inside to make sure their loud talking hadn't woken their daughter.

Her daughter was still in her bed, lying on her side, snoring lightly. Margot stared at her sweet child, suddenly breathing easier. She had a good life. She had made a good life for herself. She had everything she could ever have dreamt of, everything she had ever wanted. There was nothing to be afraid of. No one could ever take this away from her.

No one.

18

I DIDN'T SLEEP MUCH. AFTER GETTING BACK FROM THE abandoned house, I jumped into bed, but lay awake for hours afterward, wondering about what I had seen. As I realized I wasn't going to get much sleep, I grabbed my laptop instead and started a search.

As daybreak came, I had gone through a lot of old articles from forty years ago. Without eating breakfast, I rushed to the library and went to their archives as well. There, I found the rest of what I was looking for. I took photos of it all with my phone, then rushed to the Farmer's Market and had a country style breakfast. Feeling heavy after chicken and waffles, which the lady serving them said would surely *stick to my ribs*, I left the restaurant and walked back to my motel. Adeline was standing outside the front entrance and greeted me with a smile as I walked past her toward my room. I looked at my laptop and opened the email from my editor that I had received, holding my breath, praying that she would be satisfied with my article.

She wasn't.

Of course not. I knew she wouldn't be. She told me to call her, so I did.

"Was that really all you could get?" she asked. "I knew Margot Addington liked to keep her private life to herself, but still? Didn't you get anything else but this?"

I rubbed my forehead. "I'm afraid not. She was very reluctant even to talk to me, and the little she did say wasn't very impressive, to put it mildly. I just don't think she's a very interesting person with a lot to say."

"Hm, very well. The photographer will be heading over later today," she said with a sigh. "Maybe the pictures can make for an interesting feature and then we can cut the text down to a minimum. I must say, I'm not really impressed here, Rebekka."

"Neither am I," I said. I wanted to scream. I had been a journalist for all my adult life and never had I written such a terrible article. It was way below my usual standards. I so desperately wanted to prove my worth. This just wasn't my type of stuff.

"All right. I'll edit it, and then we'll run it. I've already made room for it, so there's no way around it. I sold the idea to my bosses, and they were so excited to finally hear from the mysterious Margot Addington. They're going to be very disappointed."

And I was never going to work for them again. She didn't have to say it. I knew that's what she meant.

"As I said, she wasn't very informative on anything. I got the feeling she didn't want me there at all," I said.

"I don't have to tell you that a good reporter, such as yourself, should have found an angle and kept going at it until she gave up a little something, right?"

I sighed. I just wanted to go home. "Of course."

We hung up. I wanted to throw my phone across the room and scream. Instead, I walked to my window and stared toward the abandoned house. I could see it from its back side a couple of streets down. It was a windy day, and the Spanish moss outside was fluttering in the wind. The old tree in the backyard was moving, looking like an old man trying to dance. I wondered how old that tree really was, how old the house was, and then about the story I had caught up on the night before.

A young boy had been found dead inside of that very same house, in a way eerily similar to the way Alexander Cunningham had been found. His arms were stretched out to the sides, like Jesus on the cross. And there had been writing on the wall back then too. Not when they found the body, but later on. Someone had written on the walls of the pre-school where the boy went.

I kill so that I may be eternal, it had said, just like it had the night before. And just like last night, it was believed back then to be nothing but children's pranks.

19

Leanne Peterson looked at her dress in the mirror in the hallway. She never looked good in black, she believed, and her pale face didn't make it better. Neither did the black circles under her eyes from the lack of sleep.

She sighed and looked at the picture of her son on the dresser underneath the mirror. Never would she see him in a cap and gown, graduating high school. Never would she see him find love, get married, or have children. Never was she going to see that beautiful smile again or hear his laughter again. Oh, how she had loved that laugh of his. Nothing could make her feel more pure joy than the sound of that.

"An accident," the sheriff had called it when coming to her door. "A terrible, terrible accident."

He had held his hat between his hands, Leanne had noticed. She hadn't been able to take her eyes off his fingers fiddling with it while he spoke. The sheriff's nails had been dirty.

"I am so deeply sorry for your great loss."

As she stared at the picture between her hands, thinking about the upcoming funeral and how to cope with it, there was a knock on the door. Leanne wiped a tear away, then walked to open the door. Outside stood a little girl Leanne knew lived down the street.

The girl, Anna Mae, studied Leanne, her head slightly tilted.

"Yes?" Leanne asked, wondering what the girl was doing there. "What can I help you with?"

Anna Mae grinned. "Is Timmy here?"

Leanne's eyes grew weary. She clasped her mouth and bent down with an air of deep compassion in her eyes. The poor child had no idea?

"Oh, dear. Sweet girl. I am sorry, but…" Leanne swallowed before continuing. "Haven't you heard? Timothy is dead. He died, sweetie. I'm so sorry."

Anna Mae smiled. There was something about the way the smile was crooked on one side that made Leanne's skin crawl.

"Oh, I know that he's dead."

Leanne felt confused. She stood up straight. What was this? "You knew? But…but…? I thought you…"

"I just wanted to see his dead body."

Leanne blinked. Confusion was exchanged with anger in her eyes as she slowly realized she hadn't misheard the child.

"You wanted to…what? Excuse me?"

Anna Mae was still smiling. "Do you miss him?"

Leanne shook her head. "What…what are you…why would you ask that?"

"Do you? Are you sad that he's gone?"

Leanne shook her head in confusion. "Who…who does such a thing?" she asked, appalled. Was this some sort of joke? Would a child stoop this low? "What...what are you?"

"Well, are you? Do you cry at night because you miss him so much; do you?" Anna Mae asked. It looked to Leanne like she was enjoying this.

Having had enough of this, Leanne moved away from the girl. She stared down at her, walking backward, her hands shaking. She rushed inside, then slammed the door shut. Anna Mae stood out there for a few minutes more, then turned around and walked away, skipping down the road. Leanne watched her from the window, shuddering, then picked up her phone and called Anna Mae's aunt. She knew the girl's mother, the town's local whore, would never care what she had said.

"Please, have that girl stay far away from us. Make sure she never comes to our house again, or I'll have to call the sheriff, do you hear me?"

Leanne hung up before Carol could object. She still stared at the girl in the street and didn't let her out of her sight. Anna Mae wasn't leaving; she was sitting underneath a big tree across the street as a cat walked by. The girl grabbed it by the tail and pulled it till the cat hissed. Then she let go, and it ran off hissing and wailing. Then the girl laughed.

Her husband, Tom, came up behind her. "Who was that?"

"That girl. You know, Joanna's girl," Leanne said. "She wanted to see Timothy's body. She scares me."

Tom scoffed. "She's just fooling around. Don't let her get to you."

"Do you think she did something? Do you think she might have hurt our son?" she asked.

Tom shook his head heavily. The distance between them since they got the news about Timothy seemed to be growing every day. It was like they no longer knew how to be around each other. They were secretly blaming each other for not keeping an eye on the boy, but never daring to say it out loud.

"You heard what the sheriff said that day. It was an accident," he said. "Accidents happen. I think Anna Mae is just being Anna Mae if you want my opinion."

20

I SHOULD PROBABLY HAVE GONE HOME AT THIS POINT. I WAS done with the article, it was being printed, and there was no more for me to do in Webster. Except there was. At least I felt like there was. I couldn't let go of the death of that young boy and the old story. So, instead of driving back to Cocoa Beach, I drove through town. I passed the city limit sign and entered the countryside. I drove past Lone Oak Plant Nursery, then stopped at a gated entrance to a big estate that I knew belonged to the Cucumber King. I pushed the button on the Intercom at the gate.

"Yes?" a voice asked. "Who is this?"

"My name is Rebekka Franck. I'm a reporter. I want to do a piece about your son and how he died."

"We don't talk to reporters. We're not interested," she said and was about to hang up.

"Wait, there's more. I believe these abandoned houses like the one your son went into should be demolished. That's the angle of my story. I believe it's time the local politicians wake up and take action. We need to prevent further tragedies. Demolish death-traps like the one where your son died. But I need your help; I need your story to wake them up."

Silence followed before the voice said: "When the gate opens, you take a left and follow the trail all the way to the bottom. I'm in the gray building to the right."

With those words, she disappeared. Next, the gate opened slowly, and I was let inside. I drove up the dirt road, then took a left and followed the trail. It was nice and sunny out. The rows and rows of cucumber fields lay in front of me as far as I could see.

I drove along them till I reached the end where three big gray buildings showed up. I parked in front of the one to my right and got out. The sound of voices trying to be heard over the water splashing followed as I approached the opening in the big building. Inside were maybe twenty people working. One was pouring big baskets of cucumbers onto a conveyor belt, where someone else sprayed them with water before another person picked out the bad ones and threw them away. Another conveyor belt transported them through more water, and then someone else was sorting them by size. It was like an entire factory. I spotted a woman wearing a straw hat. She was talking to one of the workers. I assumed she was Mrs. Cunningham and approached her. She finished talking to her employee, who left, then looked down at the cucumber in her gloved hand.

"It used to be citrus fruit. Did you know that?" she said. "Webster used to be real big on oranges. But then came the big freeze in 1894. All the citrus trees in the area died. Most farmers went bankrupt, except for my grandfather. He acted fast and changed to cucumbers. That was how he survived. And soon, his enterprise grew so much that they quickly gave him the nickname the Cucumber King, a name that has followed my family for generations and now belongs to my husband, who took over when my father retired. The original Cucumber King, my grandfather, was the one who started it all. He was the sole reason that Webster in the early 1900s became known as the Cucumber Capital. In 1937, a group of local farmers, with my grandfather in front, formed a co-op and without any funding from state or county, they built a market in the middle of Webster from which they could auction off their produce. And they built it themselves. They harvested cypress trees from the swamps, and it is still standing today. They used mules to drag the lumber. That's how the Farmer's Market was born."

"I see. Interesting. I read that it is now listed in the top ten attractions to visit in Florida. I've eaten at the restaurant there every day since I got here. The food is good. Solid."

Mrs. Cunningham gave me a look. She was still holding the cucumber in her hand.

"You really think you could get them to tear down that old building?"

I shrugged. "All I can do is try."

Her eyes looked into mine, and she scrutinized me. Her hand clenched the cucumber.

"That's all anyone can do, Mrs. Franck. That's all any of us can do. Follow me."

21

SHE LED ME TO A HOUSE BEHIND THE GRAY BUILDINGS, AND I guessed it was where she and the king lived. We walked onto the porch, and she told me to sit down. She took off her gloves and placed them on the patio table in front of me, then went inside. She came back a few minutes later, carrying iced tea in two glasses. She handed me one. I drank from it, then realized it was unsweetened.

"So, what is it you need from me?" she said and sat down in a rocking chair. "How can I contribute to this cause?"

I leaned forward, glass still between my hands. It felt nice and cool between my fingers. I swallowed a sip of the tea while Mrs. Cunningham rocked in the chair while using her hat as a fan. It was very hot out now, and I felt drops of sweat run down my stomach. I had dressed in too many clothes, thinking we would be inside. It was a thing that confused me often in Florida, what to wear. Outside, it was always so hot, so a little light dress would be enough, but as soon as you went inside a restaurant or someone's house, you'd freeze immediately because of the AC.

"I need your story," I said. "I need you to tell me about Alexander and about losing him. If we're to get these politicians up from their comfortable couches, we need to give them something big, something that can stir them up. A big emotional story like yours could do just that. I know it won't be easy, considering…"

I didn't get to finish the sentence before she stopped me, holding a hand in the air. She drank from her glass, then nodded.

"All right. You've got me convinced."

I nodded, thinking this was going to be tough as heck, but if I played my cards right, it could end up being quite a story. This was a story with strong emotions, and those were the ones I did best.

I grabbed my phone and used my Dictaphone app. I placed it between us on the small table.

"Tell me about Alexander. Anything that comes to mind about him. What kind of a boy was he?"

A deep silence broke out. Mrs. Cunningham was still rocking in her chair, waving air in her face. She didn't look at me, but at the fields in front of us, or the buildings next to us.

She cleared her throat.

"He was a…wonderful kid. I guess all moms say that about their sons, right?" She glanced at me briefly, then looked down at the porch again.

"Most mothers, yes," I said. "But what made him so special? What did you find to be extraordinary about him?"

She scoffed, then shook her head. "Funnily enough… his curiosity. He was always asking about everything. I sometimes got the feeling he was trying to get to know everything there was to know in this world by the time he reached eighteen and…"

Mrs. Cunningham stopped herself. I gave her time to gather her thoughts. She was never going to see him reach that age or see what he'd become. That had been robbed from her.

"As I said, he was a very curious boy."

I nodded. "They say he walked into the house on his own, probably because he thought it was an exciting place to play. Had he ever talked about the house on Second Street? Was he curious about it?"

She nodded and drank again, looking out toward the building where we had met.

"He always wanted to go in there for some reason," she said, her voice small and weary. "I had told him that it used to be an orange grove, the biggest one around here, and how they had hung those…slaves back in the old magnolia tree, back when there was that riot. He knew all the history, and he also knew that…this boy had died in there once."

"Timothy Peterson?" I asked.

She nodded. "It happened when I was just a child. An awful story. The town was never really the same again. People still don't like to talk about it. It'll probably be the same with…Alex."

"They thought it was an accident back then, right?" I asked. I glanced at the phone to make sure it was still recording everything that was being said. We were moving into the important stuff now. "But it wasn't."

She shook her head. "No. Timothy was murdered. But that was back then. It was a different story. It shook the town badly. To think that someone could…hurt such a young child was…well… Alex fell, he hurt his head, they said. It was different than back then."

"I have read many comments in the newspapers from people comparing the two stories, have you done so too?" I asked cautiously. "Do you see any similarities?"

She looked up, then put her glass down, hard. She cleared her throat again.

"Just tell them to tear that darn house down before someone else gets hurt in there, will you? Now, if you'll excuse me, I have somewhere to be. Thank you for your visit. You can let yourself out."

22

I SAT AT MY LAPTOP AND WROTE DOWN WHAT MRS. Cunningham had told me. It wasn't much yet, at least not enough for an article, but something was shaping inside of me. The way she had looked at me when mentioning the murder of Timothy Peterson had made me certain that I was onto something. This town was still licking its wounds from what had happened back then, and even though no one dared to say it out loud, it was obvious; everyone was thinking it. They were all asking themselves the same questions. *Had it happened again*? And *would it ever end*?

To answer the second question, you'd need to answer the first. And I intended to do just that. Something was off here; my intuition told me. I just couldn't figure out what.

I finished typing the interview into a Word document, then saved it for later use. Then I wrote a series of unanswered questions before closing the document and opening a browser. I stared at the blinking cursor for a few seconds, then glared down at the phone lying next to my laptop.

Sune was usually my go-to guy when it came to getting

access to places I wasn't allowed. He was the one who had done time in juvenile because of hacking when he was a teenager. He was the one who used to help me when I needed it, even if it meant him risking getting caught again. And he was good. He could get in anywhere. He would do it willingly for me because, back then, he had been crazy about me. Now, things had changed. I couldn't just call him up and ask him to break the law for me anymore.

Could I?

I held the phone between my fingers. I wondered for a few seconds what he would say if I asked.

Then I put the phone back down again. We weren't exactly acting friendly toward one another these days. Lots of ugly things had been said between us. The kind of things you couldn't just forget or easily forgive.

No, there was no way I could ask him to do this. I'd have to do it myself. Sune had taught me a lot over the past several years, and I'd have to make do with that. I wasn't a very skilled hacker just yet, but I could do stuff. Basic stuff. Over the past few years, I had improved my Linux skills, I had learned Python language, and I had learned how to use Wireshark, the most widely used protocol analyzer. Sune had taught me to understand security concepts and technologies. Teaching me the basics of PKI—public key infrastructure, SSL—secure sockets layer, IDS—intrusion detection system, firewalls, and so on.

I had practiced my skills using Virtualbox, which was a virtualization software where you created a safe environment to practice your hacks before taking them to the real world. But I had never done anything real. Not yet at least.

I took in a deep breath, remembering Sune's advice that a good hacker always thought outside the box. It was all about making a system work in ways it was not designed to.

So, I did. I found the medical examiner's database through the sheriff's office. At first, I tried to get access the obvious way. I used admin login and tried to guess the password, using a webpage a famous hacker had created with options. I tried a lot of different combinations, but it was no use. Then, I ran a password-auditing tool, and bingo, after a couple of hours at it, I had gained access.

I smiled and was about to grab my phone to call and tell Sune, thinking he was going to be so excited when I stopped myself. That wasn't the kind of relationship we had.

Not anymore.

I looked through the database, then searched for Alexander Cunningham's name and found the medical examiner's report and the autopsy.

It was almost too easy. Sweat prickling on my forehead, and slightly satisfied with my own skills, I skimmed through it, then took pictures of the screen with my phone, making sure to get all the pages. I then hurried and got back out again before anyone noticed I had been there. If there was one thing Sune had taught me it was to cover my tracks. I always masked my IP, and I always cleared the history on my computer afterward. And I never ever bragged about what I had done. Many hackers were caught from bragging on Twitter. Twitter attached GPS coordinates to photo uploads by default. It was important never to leave a trace they could follow, Sune had taught me, along with everything he believed that I needed to know about digital forensics.

Satisfied, I closed the lid on my computer, then opened

the documents on my phone and started to read. Reading an autopsy was more on my turf. I knew how to read between the lines and to distinguish between what was important and what wasn't.

And what I found on the very first page was very important indeed.

23

I SPENT MOST OF THE FOLLOWING DAY ON THE PHONE. I called every editor I knew or had heard of, trying to sell my story. But no one wanted it. It wasn't until I reached an editor at *Florida Today* and told her about what I had found that I sensed an opening.

"If you can prove a crime has been committed, then, yes, we'll buy it," she said. "If it turns out to be connected to the murder forty years ago, then you have yourself a national story in *USA Today*."

I hung up with a sense of eagerness inside me. I could smell that there was a scoop here somewhere. I just had to find a way to dig it out. I grabbed my phone and called Sune as I drove to the Farmer's Market for lunch.

"I need to stay a little longer," I said. "I can't come home yet. Can you keep the kids for a few more days?"

"What? What are you talking about? You can't do that, Rebekka," he said. "I have a life too, you know?"

"I've been gone three days. I think you can take the kids for two more days if needed. I fell upon another story while I was here. *Florida Today* will run it. But it will take a little while. It's a lot of money, though, and that will mean that I won't have to work for weeks."

Sune went silent. "Exactly what kind of a story are we talking about? Is it another interview or…?"

I sighed and parked in front of the old wooden building with the four rocking chairs on the porch. A little girl sat in one of them, rocking back and forth with a small dog in her lap. I spotted Adeline coming out with a friend, holding a box of leftovers in her hand.

"They found the body of a boy inside an abandoned house. They say he was killed in an accident, but…"

"Ah here we go again," he said exhaling. "You don't believe it's an accident, am I right?"

"Listen to me, Sune. It's not just something I've come up with out of the blue. There was another boy. He was also found dead in the exact same spot forty years ago."

"Geez, Rebekka, you think you see a story in everything. Can you never just let something go? It could be a coincidence and, once you realize that, you'll have wasted all this time and my time as well."

"I don't believe in coincidences; you know that." I paused, feeling tired. I hated the way Sune and I spoke to one another now. I wanted to ask him how his training was going, ask him how he was doing, if he had enjoyed being out on his first photographer job again. I longed to connect with him, like really connect and talk about important stuff. Back in the day, we would work on a story like this together, and I could use him to bounce off my theories and ideas. How did that disappear from one day to the next? I hadn't just lost my boyfriend and the father of my second child. I had lost my best friend.

You're the one who threw him out, remember? You didn't want him back. Even though he cried and asked for forgiveness. You told

him to go be with Kim. You said that you and he were done. You prac-
tically threw him back into her arms.

"Listen, I gotta go. Tell the kids I love them and that I'll call later."

I didn't wait for his reply but hung up. I wiped a tear from the corner of my eye, then got out of the car, my stomach rumbling loudly.

Adeline and her friend were still on the porch, chatting. I approached them near the door.

"Ah, Rebekka," Adeline said. "How are you on this fine day?"

"I'm well, thank you," I lied. I wasn't doing very well, to be honest. I felt crushed and missed having Sune in my life. "I'm just about to grab something to eat."

"Their cornbread is to die for," she smiled. "Rebekka is the reporter I told you about," Adeline said, addressed to her friend standing next to her. She had short curly hair that went down beneath her ears and very blue eyes.

The woman smiled. "I see. How interesting."

"I'm doing a story about Margot Addington, the author," I said. "I had an interview with her yesterday."

They both looked like they had no idea who she was.

"She actually lives closer to Bushnell. On a farm about ten to fifteen miles from here."

"What type of books does she write?" the curly-haired woman asked.

"Mysteries," I said. "The latest, *The Terrible Death of Angus McMannus*, is currently number one on the *NYT* best-seller list. It's quite good."

The women both shuddered. "I never read that stuff," the small woman with the curls said. "It's too realistic if you ask me. Gives me nightmares."

"If she's a local girl, then maybe we should read it, just

to say we knew her," Adeline said. "I've never heard her name before, though."

"Well, she's a newcomer," I said. "Moved here only four years ago with her husband and daughter. He is a neurosurgeon at Leesburg Regional. Theodore Addington."

Adeline shook her head. "Never heard of him either."

The door opened, and a man stepped out. I recognized him as the mayor of Webster, Mayor Pickens. He was chewing on a toothpick and smiling a satisfied smile at Adeline and the curly-haired woman before lifting his hat with a sturdy, "Hello, ladies." The smell coming from inside made my stomach scream for food.

"Well, maybe you should check her out one day. She's quite good. Now, if you'll excuse me, I have to get something to eat before I explode."

"Get the fried chicken," Adeline said, holding my hand in hers briefly while smiling. I smiled back.

"Will do. See you ladies later."

24

STOMACH FILLED AND FEELING MORE AT EASE, I LEFT THE Farmer's Market, then drove back to the motel. I still had a lot of research to do and, even though everything did seem brighter after the big meal, I still felt a little discouraged. I didn't really know how to go about this story. How to get into it.

As I parked the car, I received a text from Julie.

HAVING A TERRIBLE DAY.

Oh, no.

WHAT'S GOING ON?

I DON'T HAVE ANY FRIENDS.

WHAT HAPPENED TO YOUR FRIENDS?

THEY ALL HATE ME. NO ONE IS TALKING TO ME. I AM ALL ALONE.

I sighed and rubbed my eyes in frustration. I hated that I couldn't do anything to help her. Middle school was just terrible.

YOU'LL BE OKAY, I wrote back, not knowing what else to say. YOU CAN FIND NEW FRIENDS?

I DON'T WANT NEW FRIENDS.

I knew what she meant. She had one very good friend, Maggie, whom she always hung out with, but every now and then, Maggie would rather hang out with Kylie than Julie, and that left my daughter all alone. I didn't understand why they couldn't just hang out all three of them, but apparently, that wasn't a solution.

SCHOOL IS OVER IN A FEW HOURS. TOMORROW, IT'LL ALL BE BETTER, I tried, even though I knew it wouldn't comfort Julie.

I MISS YOU. WHEN ARE YOU COMING HOME?

And there it was. The nagging feeling of guilt. Not only did Julie have to deal with friend trouble but she also had to miss her mother and be with her ex-stepdad and his new girlfriend instead. I felt terrible.

IN A COUPLE OF DAYS, I replied. I'LL CALL LATER. I LOVE YOU.

LOVE YOU TOO.

I exhaled and put the phone in my pocket. I got out of the car, then slammed the door shut when someone approached me, rushing toward me so fast I could barely react.

"Who the hell do you think you are?" he hissed at me.

"Excuse me? I don't even know who you are."

The man standing in front of me in cowboy boots was tall and intimidating. The shirt he was wearing was expensive. So was his leather hat. I recognized him from the photo I had seen in the newspapers.

Mark Cunningham, Alexander's dad, aka the current Cucumber King.

His red-rimmed eyes glared at me angrily. "Why would you do such a thing?"

I stared at him, confused. I was pressed up against the car to keep my distance from him and his agitated hands.

"Do what exactly? I'm not sure I follow."

"My wife. Why would you be putting those ideas in her head?"

"I'm not sure I understand. What ideas?" I asked, wondering if I still had that pepper spray in my bag Sune once gave me for situations like these. I wasn't one to own a gun, so he told me always to carry that instead. Just in case.

Mark Cunningham's nostrils were flaring. He pointed his finger at me, his eyes on fire.

"I'm telling you…you…you stay out of this. Alexander's death was an accident. I don't need you comin' here and tellin' my wife otherwise; do you hear me?"

He spoke through gritted teeth. I could see his jaw moving behind the skin. "I…I never meant to…"

He stepped closer. I could smell his breath on my face. "I think it's best you leave town now. You hear me? We don't want people like you here. You're not welcome anymore."

"Excuse me?" I asked, startled. "Are you threatening me?"

He slammed his hand brusquely into the roof of my car. "We don't need no nosy little reporter comin' here and messing with our heads. You get out of here, now. You hear me? Pack your little things and leave."

I couldn't believe my own ears. I stared at the man, my heart throbbing in my chest. He snorted at me, spat on the ground next to me, then turned around on his heel and trotted back toward his pick-up truck. Seconds later, the engine roared, and he drove out of the parking lot, his tires screeching as he turned onto the road and took off.

I stood there, my heart pounding in my chest, staring after him, completely baffled.

Once I couldn't see the truck anymore, I got back into my own car and took off.

25

Webster, Florida 1979

Carol stood outside her sister's house when she heard something fall and break. As usual, she hated coming to her sister's place. It was so dirty and disgusting; Carol tried never to touch anything. She never knew who was inside the house, if her sister was working or not, so she knocked and waited for her sister to open the door. She never just knocked and then walked inside, as most people did around there. Not in this house. You never knew what you'd find on the other side.

"Joanna?" she said as she heard the loud thud. More bumps followed, sounding like someone was struggling.

Carol swallowed and looked at the door handle. Did she dare to walk in? She had done it once before when she thought her sister was in trouble, then found her on the kitchen table, a strange man on top of her. Her sister had laughed when she saw Carol's terrified face.

Was this like that time? If so, then she wouldn't go in. She'd wait outside.

But what if she was really in trouble this time? What if she needed her help? What if Anna Mae did?

She had come to talk to Joanna because she was worried about Anna Mae. They had called from the Petersons' house and told her that Anna Mae had been standing outside of their house when the coffin of little Timothy was carried out. She had a grin on her face, Leanne had said. Leanne had tried desperately to get Anna Mae to stop coming by, to stop asking if she missed Timothy. Leanne had stopped opening the door if she knocked, but she still knew she was out there, ready to torment her. She couldn't take it, Leanne had said, crying.

Carol had tried to make excuses for the girl. She said she was just fascinated by what had happened, that maybe you couldn't blame her for being a little strange with everything that went on in her own house.

But now, Leanne was threatening to call the police, and that could turn out to be trouble for Anna Mae if she didn't stop it. She had to stay away from the Petersons' house from now on. Carol hoped that by telling Joanna this, that maybe she might step up and be a mother for once.

"Don't get your hopes up too high, Carol." That's what John had said to her this same morning when she told him her intentions.

Another thud sounded from behind the door, and then a small scream followed. Carol knew she couldn't just stand there anymore. She had to do something. So, she did. She grabbed the handle and turned it, then opened the door, bracing herself for what she'd find on the other side.

But what she saw, she had no way of preparing herself for. No one would. Anna Mae was on the floor, a man on top of her, in this instant pulling his pants down to his knees. Anna Mae was trying to get out from underneath him, but he was holding her down. Meanwhile, her mother stood leaned up against the counter, smoking a cigarette, looking at them like she couldn't care less what happened to her daughter.

"What on Earth…? Joanna?" Carol shrieked. Then she spotted a stack of money on the kitchen counter, and suddenly she felt like throwing up. "Did you…did you…?"

She couldn't even get herself to say the words. She stared at Anna Mae crying on the floor. The big man on top of her wasn't getting off. He was trying to kiss her, forcing his stubbled face at her.

"What are you doing to her?" Carol screamed. "What have you done?" She grabbed the man and tried to pull him off her, but he didn't move.

Then she ran to the stove, grabbed a pan, and with a scream worthy of an Amazon warrior, she ran toward him. As the man saw her, he let go of Anna Mae. He got up and began to run, tripping on his pants that he fought to pull back up.

"Crazy bitch," he hissed, then rushed outside and, seconds later, he was gone.

Carol turned to look at her sister, trying to say something, but no words left her mouth.

"You…you sold her?" she finally managed to ask. "You sold your own daughter like she was some…sex slave?"

Her sister blew out smoke. "Yeah, well, I guess you just ruined that."

"I sure hope so," Carol said. She couldn't believe her sister's indifference. How could she not care what happened to her only child?

Anna Mae was still crying, and Carol took her in her arms. She carried her toward the door.

"She's coming home with me," she said, her eyes flat with determination. "And she'll be staying there. If you object, I'll tell the sheriff everything, and you'll be sent to jail."

She didn't wait for her sister to answer. She turned around and carried Anna Mae out of there, her heart aching.

26

THE SHERIFF'S OFFICE WAS LOCATED NEXT TO CITY HALL. I found Sheriff Travers sitting behind his desk, eating—not surprisingly—a piece of pie, trying to keep in shape for the competition, I guessed.

The door was open, so I just walked inside. His face grew gloomy as he spotted me. He leaned back and forced a smile.

"You again? I'm surprised to see that you're still around?"

I lifted my eyebrows. "I would like to file a report against Mark Cunningham. He just threatened me in the parking lot in front of the motel."

Sheriff Travers stared at me, his hands meeting at the top of his stomach. The cup in front of him read:

BEST FRIGGIN' SHERIFF EVER.

"He did, now, did he?"

"He sure did. He told me to leave town."

"Did anyone witness this threat being made?"

"I don't think so."

"And what exactly was he threatening you with?"

"He didn't say," I said. "But he was being very aggressive toward me."

The sheriff's leather chair creaked as he moved forward. "So, you want to report for him threatening you with nothing?"

I exhaled. "He was being threatening toward me. He told me to leave town."

The sheriff nodded. "Okay. Fill out the paperwork by the front desk, and I'll look into it. When I have the time."

"Why do I have the feeling that won't be anytime soon?" I asked.

He threw out his arms. "We're very busy. Lot's of paperwork recently. Some of it might even get lost. You know how it is."

I clenched my fist, annoyed. I don't know what I had expected by coming there, but it was the best idea I had been able to come up with. I wasn't going to let some buffoon threaten me and not do anything about it, even if that buffoon did own half the town. I didn't like this guy one bit. He was a man who looked like he had a lot on his conscience, like he was hiding something big.

"Anything else?" the sheriff asked. He glanced at the piece of pie next to him, and I could tell he couldn't wait to dig back in.

I was about to walk away when I stopped myself. "As a matter of fact, there is."

The sheriff grinned. "Why doesn't that surprise me?"

I placed my hands on his desk, then leaned across it. "There was something that had me wondering. When I spoke to Mrs. Cunningham, Alexander Cunningham's mother, she told me the boy died from falling, from hurting his head. But the autopsy report doesn't mention any bruises to his head. According to it, he died from asphyxiation. Now, there were no bruises on his throat to indicate he was strangled, but he sure didn't die from falling. Why would you tell the parents that?"

The sheriff went quiet, and his smile froze in place. He stared at me, his nostrils flaring lightly, a vein popping out on his throat.

"And just how—pray tell—do you know what the autopsy report states?" he asked. "I don't recall you being next of kin or even requesting access to the report. Because I would have denied it to you."

"Why did you lie to them? Why not tell the parents the truth?" I asked.

The sheriff gritted his teeth. "I think it's best you leave now. For both of us."

I didn't budge. "Why did you lie to them? Is it because you're afraid the killer is back? Because you fear it's the same person that killed Timothy Peterson forty years ago? Is that it?"

The sheriff rose to his feet with a grunt. He pointed at the door.

"GET OUT."

27

MOST PEOPLE DIDN'T NOTICE HER, BUT SHE WAS USED TO that. As a homeless person, she was used to slipping in and out of places unseen. And so she did again on this late afternoon. She slipped unseen into the Circle K just for a few minutes to cool down. It was so hot out that she felt like she was going to melt. She needed to feel the cold air on her face for just a second.

She had left her belongings outside on a bench. There was hardly anything in them, so she wasn't afraid they would be stolen. But she couldn't take the bags with her since people would be able to tell she was homeless.

Ah, the smell of hot dogs.

The woman stared at the food by the counter, the hot dogs turning and sizzling. She felt the hunger nagging in her stomach, then turned away. She had no money. She had stayed at the intersection by Wal-Mart most of the day, but no one had mercy on her and slipped her any bills. She reached inside the pocket of her dirty pants that she had stolen from a guy who had been sleeping on a cardboard box under a bridge. He had a bag of clothes in a shopping cart next to him, and she slipped the pants out, not realizing they were way too hot for this weather. But in the wintertime, she would have good use of them, if they lasted that long. If you had to choose a place to be homeless, Florida was a good place since the winters didn't get very cold, but boy, the summers were tough when you couldn't find shelter from the sun and the heat.

The woman closed her eyes and walked closer to the vent where the cold air came out. She let it fall on her face for a few seconds; then, when she opened them again, the manager was standing in front of her. She knew him from the many times he had thrown her out before. She wasn't allowed to use their restroom anymore since he said it was only for paying costumers.

"You buying anything today?" he asked. "Did you bring any money?"

She grinned. Then she held up the dollar in front of his young face. "I sure am. Can I get one of those hot dogs, please?"

The manager looked displeased, then grabbed her dollar and walked behind the counter.

"Give her a hot dog so she'll get out of here," he said to the teenager behind it. The young man gave her a look of disgust, then grabbed a hot dog and put it in a bun. The manager put the dollar away, and the woman took the hot dog. She smelled it before taking the first bite, then gobbled it down.

"Now, you can leave," the manager said as a young couple entered, looking shiny and full of money.

"I'm a paying customer," she said and chewed. "I'm entitled to be here. Afterward, I'll need to use your restroom too."

The manager was about to protest but knew he couldn't. He sighed instead and left her with a growl. The young couple looked at the magazines by the counter, then grabbed one and paid for it.

The woman chewed while watching them buy sodas and candy. She watched a wallet go back into a back pocket. Just in the right place to be picked.

The woman grinned to herself when her eyes fell on the magazine the woman was now holding in her hands. Then, she froze.

That picture on the front cover!

She rushed to the magazines and grabbed one for herself, flipping through the pages until she found the article.

"Hey, you have to pay for that if you want to read it," the manager yelled at her. "This isn't a library, you know."

But the woman didn't move. She kept reading the article, word for word, and then she placed her finger on the byline and the small picture next to it, "Rebekka Franck," she mumbled to herself, grinning widely. Then she ripped out a page of the article while the manager yelled at her.

"HEY!"

The manager pulled the magazine out of her hands and then told her to leave. The woman smiled at him, then rushed toward the sliding doors, the ripped-out page clutched in her hand, thinking she was going to be back as soon as she had found this woman. And by then, the manager would have to take a much nicer tone with her because she intended to come back rich.

28

SHE HADN'T BEEN ABLE TO WRITE A SINGLE SENTENCE FOR days. Margot Addington wasn't feeling well. She wasn't sleeping, and she was hardly eating. She was worried about the article coming out. What kind of picture had the reporter painted of her? Would she be able to recognize herself?

"Your tea is getting cold, honey. You haven't even touched it."

Margot jumped at the sound of her husband's voice. She looked down at the teacup sitting on the table in front of her. The tea bag was still in it, the small string hanging from the side. It wasn't steaming anymore. It wasn't even warm to the touch. How long had she been sitting there?

"Have you been sitting there all day?" Theodore asked. "You were in that exact same spot when I left this morning. You haven't even cleaned up after breakfast. You usually always do that. Are you sick?"

Theodore felt her forehead. "You don't have a fever, but that doesn't mean you aren't sick."

Margot smiled. "I'm fine. I just have a lot on my mind. I'll clean up later."

He sighed and sat down. "What's going on with you? Is it still that silly interview? I told you it doesn't matter what they write. We don't have to care."

Margot cleared her throat. She wanted to speak, but no words left her lips, simply because she didn't really know what to say. Fact was, she felt terrified. That was why she never did interviews. She knew she should never have done this one either, that it would end up torturing her. She should have listened to her intuition.

He placed his hand on top of hers and squeezed it. "I'm sure it'll be fine. You said that the reporter seemed nice, right?"

The front door slammed shut, and Minna came rushing in, holding a magazine in her hand.

"Got it!"

She threw it casually on the table in front of Margot. Margot gasped when she saw her own picture on the cover. Her own two blue eyes were staring back at her, almost accusingly, like they were saying: *You don't belong here. You don't deserve this.*

"I think you look great, Mom," her daughter said. "No, make that awesome. You look like you should be a model."

"That is a gorgeous photo," Theodore said. "Don't you think?"

Margot nodded, unable to speak. She reached out and grabbed the magazine, then opened it, finding the article. She read through it, her heart pounding in her chest as she felt herself being unveiled word by word.

Then, she breathed in relief. It wasn't too bad. The article was only a third of it; the rest was just pictures. Even though Margot didn't like seeing herself on display like this, she was pleased that the article had been good.

Theodore put his hand on her shoulder. "I told you there was nothing to worry about."

Margot smiled for the first time in days. Her shoulders came down, and she felt relaxed.

"It did come out pretty good, didn't it?"

"Pretty good?" Minna asked. "I think it's awesome. You look so beautiful. I am really proud to be your daughter right now."

Margot breathed in. She felt how the relief rushed through her body and made every muscle relax. It wasn't the end of the world after all. She could breathe again now. She could return to her writing again, return to normalcy.

It was over.

29

I WAS SO ANGRY. I DROVE BACK TO THE MOTEL AND LET myself into my room, my blood boiling. Out of the window, I looked at the water tower with WEBSTER written on the side. What was it with this town that gave me the creeps? Something was very wrong here, I believed; something was completely off. Why were Mark Cunningham and the sheriff both so eager to get rid of me? Why was the sheriff lying? Did Mark Cunningham know that his son didn't die from a fall? Was he in on the lie?

It would explain why he got mad at me for talking to his wife about the similarities to the death of Timothy Peterson. But it didn't explain why he was in such a rush for his wife to believe it was an accident. What did he gain from that? Had he killed his own son? And Timothy? But he couldn't have been much more than a kid himself back then. What was his deal? Could it be to protect his wife? But why? So she wouldn't know the boy had been killed?

It made no sense.

I opened my laptop and went through my notes, then

looked at the pictures of the autopsy report I had taken, scrolling through all the pictures of the body lying on the floor. I compared it to the picture from an old newspaper from '79 where they had made a drawing of the way the body had been found.

Looking at the two of them, I had no doubt. It was exactly the same. They hadn't fallen; they had been placed. And for some reason, the sheriff was covering it up.

I leaned back in my seat, wondering what I could do with this information. It was all speculation so far. I couldn't really run with what I had found in the autopsy report since it wasn't made public. I couldn't use any of it without having to explain how I got it. I thought for a minute about asking for an interview with the chief medical examiner but then decided against it. He wouldn't be allowed to say much if he was even allowed to meet up with me. I could request to see the autopsy, but the sheriff would probably deny that to me or just make sure it was delayed so much that I would never get it.

Then what? What could I possibly go after? I had the short interview with Alexander Cunningham's mother, but that was barely news if the boy had just fallen. The paper had said they weren't interested in the angle about the abandoned houses and how they ought to be demolished. It wasn't interesting enough. I had to prove somehow that Alexander was murdered.

I fiddled with my phone between my fingers, looking out at the town from my window. Cars rushed by on Market Boulevard. No one spoke of Alexander anymore. I hadn't heard anyone talk about him when eating lunch. There had been no flowers placed in front of the old house. Why was this town in such a hurry to forget?

As long as they believe it's an accident, they can move on. Acci-

dents happen. The boy did something foolish, and it was tragic, yes, but tragedies happen.

Was that why the sheriff was in such a rush to call it an accident? Because he feared for the town's reaction?

I found the copies of the old articles from '79 and read through them. People had been outraged back then, and they had demanded answers. They had gathered in front of the police station once it was revealed that Timothy didn't die by accident. They had demanded that the sheriff stop the killer and make sure it didn't happen again.

But my question was. How was it suddenly revealed that it was no accident? How did they find out?

I had barely finished the thought when there was a knock on my door. I went to open it, taking in a deep breath first, and peeking through the window to make sure it wasn't Mark Cunningham coming back to make sure I had left and forcing me to when realizing I hadn't.

It was an old woman in rags. Relieved, I let my shoulders down, then walked to open the door.

30

It was a local journalist who made all hell break loose in their town. Until then, everyone had believed little Timothy had simply fallen and hurt himself when playing inside the old abandoned house. They had shaken their heads and called it a tragedy, but one that could have been avoided had the parents only kept a proper eye on the boy.

But along came a journalist from the local *Webster Daily* and ruined it all. One day, he had lunch with the chief medical examiner and, as the lunch progressed, the drinks piled up, and soon the medical examiner started to spill out.

"Timothy didn't fall. He had no bruises to match a fall. He suffocated," he said. And then he added what later became the thing that most people talked about:

"My guess is he was strangled. The only reason there are no bruises on his neck is that the killer was most likely a child. Their fingers are small and won't leave bruises as they press on the child's throat."

That last remark was what soon had the entire town on

its feet. Carol watched from a distance as they gathered in front of the sheriff's office, yelling for him to take action. People were holding up their children, asking if they were going to be next.

"Children killing children," her best friend Adeline said, shaking her head as she approached her. "What will it be next?"

"They don't know that for sure," Carol said. "Just because some drunk doctor said so in an interview. I don't believe a word of it. Timothy fell down and killed himself."

"He did the autopsy of little Timmy. I think he knows what he saw," she said. "Don't you? You think that you know better than him?"

Carol shrugged. She glanced toward her house where Anna Mae was waiting for her to return. She had started homeschooling the girl to make sure she stayed away from the many staring eyes and didn't have to deal with the bullies calling her and her mother whores or even whispering about her in the hallways. She was trying to give the girl as ordinary an upbringing as possible.

She knew what people thought about Anna Mae. Especially now that this had come out. This morning, they had woken up to eggs being thrown at their windows and then, as Carol ran outside, she saw the word *Killer* painted on the garage door. She had spent hours washing it off, but you could still see it. Kids were calling and yelling at her that she was a killer and some even said it to her face.

Only Anna Mae's friend Bella would still come over and hang out with her. She wasn't a very bright kid, so Carol assumed that she just didn't understand what was going on. But she welcomed her and always made sure Bella felt at home when she visited. It was healthy for Anna Mae to have friends. If only the world could be a warmer place.

"Did you hear about the painting?" Adeline said.

"No," Carol said. "What painting?"

"Someone broke into the pre-school and painted on the walls last night. In Timmy's classroom. They wrote *I kill that I may be eternal*, or something like that, using red paint. The police said it was just pranksters, but I think it was the killer who did it. To let us all know that he—or she —did it."

As Adeline said the last sentence, she glanced toward Carol's house where Anna Mae was standing in the window, looking out.

Carol thought for a second about the night before, when Anna Mae had come home late. She had been out playing with Bella and forgot the time, she said. Carol shook her head. No, there was no way Anna Mae had written those words. Bella would have told her if she did. She could never keep quiet about anything, the stupid girl.

It couldn't be her. Not her Anna Mae.

31

THE WOMAN STANDING OUTSIDE MY DOOR SMILED BEHIND A weathered face. My guess was that she looked older than she really was. Her clothes were ragged, and she smelled terrible. In her hands, she was holding two plastic bags, and I wondered if that was all her belongings.

My first thought was that she was begging for money, so I reached into the pocket of my shorts to search for a bill.

"Are you Rebekka Franck?" she asked, grinning. "The woman who wrote the article in the magazine?"

I stopped the search, realizing she had come to see me in person, not just knocked randomly at my door.

"Yes?" I said. "Can I help you with anything?"

"I read your article. The one about the author."

I smiled. I had seen it at the Circle K earlier when going for a coffee. The cover picture was gorgeous. I had bought myself a copy, and it was lying next to my laptop. The article I still felt a little disappointed about, but the way the editor had mixed it up with the pictures from her farm, the horses and her workplace, it had come out okay, I thought.

"Well, I'm glad you read it," I said, thinking she was just some reader who wanted to let me know she had enjoyed the article. Usually, people would shoot me an email and let me know, not come to my door. "Did you like it?"

She smiled from ear to ear. Her teeth were chipped and dirty. "Oh, I liked it. I liked it very much."

"Well, that's great then," I said. This woman wasn't exactly the target group for the magazine that was usually read by a young and fashionable audience, so I was a little surprised she would have read it. It was quite expensive too, and she didn't look like she could afford to spend that amount of money on something as inessential as a magazine filled with fashion and interviews with famous people. Maybe she found it somewhere? Someone left it behind on a bench?

"I'm glad you enjoyed it," I said and was about to end the conversation. But the woman kept staring at me like she wanted something else from me. I tried to get rid of her.

"Now, if you'll excuse me, I have more work to do."

I was about to close the door when she put her foot in it and slammed her hands on it to stop me.

I gave her a strange look. "Was there something else I could do for you?"

She nodded. "Yes, as a matter of fact, there is."

I exhaled, getting a little tired of this. I had lots of articles I needed to read.

"Okay, then. What can I do for you?"

"The question is what I can do for you."

I was beginning to feel a little uncomfortable in this

woman's presence. She was standing a little too close to me for my liking, and I pulled back.

"I have a story for ya'," she then said, her southern accent turning heavy. "A good one."

I looked at my watch. I had promised Julie I would call her when she got back from school. I didn't really have time for some crazy woman and her stories.

"Maybe you can write a letter to the magazine?" I asked. "They're really the ones who decide what to publish and not to publish. I just do the interview and write the article once it is decided. If they like your idea, then they'll definitely run it."

She shook her head. "No. This story is for you and you'll want this. Believe me."

There was something about the way she said it that intrigued me. She reached inside a pocket and pulled out a piece of crumpled up paper, then unfolded it and held it up for me to see.

Margot Addington was staring back at me.

"It's about her," she said and pointed at Margot's nose. "I have a story about her, and I'm willing to give it to you before anyone else. It's a story that will rock your world."

I stared at the picture of the elegant Margot Addington in her long black dress standing on the wooden floors of her house, looking like a movie star from the thirties. I wondered about the interview and how little she had wanted to give me, and how disappointed I had been. Could this woman really have something?

I then looked into the eyes of the strange woman in front of me, smiling from ear to ear, weighing my options. This woman might just be crazy and what she had could be nothing, but if I turned her down now, she'd go some-where else, and I'd miss out on what could be a great story.

"Okay, you have my attention. Come on in," I said and opened the door.

32

THE WOMAN PRESENTED HERSELF AS JOANNA. HER EYES lingered on me as I grabbed a chair for her to sit on. I sat across from her, the laptop next to me, the phone ready to record what she had to say.

Stories coming out of the blue like this were rarely anything newsworthy, but every now and then, you could stumble across something that would be worth spending your time on.

I was hoping this would be one of those times.

I grabbed my notepad and a pen, then sat with it on my lap. "Okay. I'm listening. What's your story?"

She placed the picture of Margot on the desk and smoothed it out. Then she pointed at her.

"That woman there…"

"Margot Addington, the author," I said.

"Yes."

"What about her?" I asked.

Joanna smiled again.

"She's a killer," she said. "A vicious murderer."

And there you have it. The woman is full-blown crazy. Face it. You're wasting your time, Rebekka. Time you don't have.

"And what exactly makes you say that? Do you have anything to back up this assertion?" I asked, beginning to fear that this woman was delusional. I had met my fair share of conspiracy theorists and strange people with a story to tell in my life. As a reporter, you had to get used to it. Everywhere you went, people would come up to you with a good story they believed you needed to write. One they thought was more important than anything else. It didn't matter if you were at a dinner party somewhere or just grocery shopping. Everyone had a story.

"Because I know this. I know that is what she is, even if she's trying to run from it."

I smiled politely, looking discretely at my watch. I hoped Julie wasn't too upset that I hadn't called her yet. I couldn't believe I was wasting my time listening to this woman instead of talking to my beloved daughter.

"And how do you know this? How do you know Margot Addington?" I asked.

Joanna grinned. "Wouldn't you like to know?"

I sighed, thinking this had been a mistake. "Well, if you can't tell me, then there's no story for me to tell. I need to make sure you're a reliable source and not just someone out to hurt her."

"Ask her about it," she said. "Ask her if she didn't kill little Timmy forty years ago. Ask her if she didn't strangle him to death inside that old house on Second Street."

Now, she had my interest. Little Timmy could only be Timothy Peterson, the boy whose murder I was investigating.

"Timothy Peterson?" I asked.

She nodded eagerly. "Yes, yes. That's the one."

"But why would you say that Margot Addington killed

him? As far as I know, she's from Missouri and could only have been about ten years old back then. She was only a child."

Joanna leaned forward. "Children can kill."

I cleared my throat, remembering what I had just read in the article about the chief medical examiner back in '79 and what he had told the journalist. I bit my cheek while wondering if this woman was just mad or if I should take her seriously. It didn't add up, though.

"But she grew up in Missouri, " I repeated. "She told me so when I did the interview."

Joanna shook her head and pointed at the picture once again. "This girl grew up here in Webster. Right down the street from here. She went to Webster Elementary School like all the other children around here. She climbed the same trees they all did, and she's a killer; I tell ya'. She can't run from that. She murdered that child using her bare hands. She's a cruel, cruel killer and now she has struck again."

I looked at my notes, then up at the woman. I wasn't sure she was completely sane.

"I'm sorry; I don't really know how to…" I said feeling tired. "How do you know all this?"

Joanna leaned forward. Her breath smelled like alcohol and cigarettes as she spoke.

"She can change the way she looks. She can change her name; she can change anything she wants to, but a momma always knows her baby when she sees her. And this woman here is no Margot Addington. Her name is Anna Mae Burke. I know this because I gave her that name. I know this because I am her mother. Now, do you want this story or not? 'Cause it'll have to cost ya'. I need you to pay up if you want the rest."

Joanna leaned forward, grabbed the pen from my hand, then wrote a number on my pad.

"That's what I want. This is what it'll cost 'ya. But it'll be worth every penny; believe me."

I leaned back in my chair with an exhale. "I'm sorry. I'm afraid you've come to the wrong person. I don't pay my sources for stories. That's not how I work. Besides, I don't have the kind of money that you're asking."

"But...but you have to. This is my price. Surely, that magazine you work for will pay? They have plenty of money; just call them up and tell them that you have a great story that they need to run."

I shook my head. "I'm just a freelance reporter; I have no say in what they run and don't run. And, to be honest, I don't think a magazine like that will pay for such a story. They're not into sensational stories like that. You'll want to contact the tabloids, and I don't write for them."

Joanna's face froze, then she rose to her feet.

"Then I'll go somewhere else, but you'll be sorry that you didn't take this story when I offered it to you. It could have been yours."

"Go ahead. It's a free country," I said and watched as the woman rushed out the door without even a word to thank me for taking my time. As the door slammed shut, I placed my pad on the desk, wondering if anyone else would bite onto that story. If so, then Margot Addington was in for quite a storm. There was nothing the tabloids loved more than the story of the fall of someone considered to be great.

I, for one, would have no part of a story like that. This woman had to have some sort of grudge against Margot; that would be the only explanation. Or maybe she was just crazy. I wasn't out to smear anyone or destroy their lives based on loose rumors or crazy people telling stories. Besides, I didn't believe anything of what she told me. There was no way Margot Addington had ever hurt anyone in her life. I simply refused to believe it.

33

MARGOT ADDINGTON LAUGHED. NOT THAT FAKE LAUGHTER that she had taught herself for charity events or when invited to fancy dinners with Theodore's colleagues and they said some joke only surgeons would understand. No, this was real laughter. This was real joy.

They were sitting around the coffee table in the living room, all three of them, playing Monopoly. Minna threw the dice and moved her figure. Then she looked at her mother triumphantly.

"I'll buy this one, and next time you land here, I'll ruin you."

Margot smiled. It felt so good just to sit there and be. Just be with her family, the two people she loved so dearly. Next to them lay the magazine. She had read the article over and over again, each time filled with more and more relief and joy. This hadn't been as bad as she had feared, not at all. As she read through it the third time, she had actually thought she had come out sounding quite intelligent, and she had remained mysterious.

Edward, her agent, had called earlier and told her he

was proud of it, and so was the publishing house. And the sales were already feeling it. Today, she had sold more books than the past week altogether. So, it wasn't just good; it was excellent.

The only fear that still lingered in Margot was that now they'd ask her to do a lot more interviews. Now that they knew she could do them, that she could be pressured into doing them, it might not end here. But Margot had decided she wouldn't. This was the last one she'd ever do. Her agent and her publisher would have to live with that. It hadn't been worth it. It had almost torn her apart inside, and she never wanted to feel like that again. She didn't want to sell off her soul one interview at a time because that was how it would go. Each journalist would take it a little further, would want a little more of her, would want another story, one that was better than the previous one, and in the end, there would be nothing of Margot left.

She couldn't risk that happening.

"It's your turn, dear," Theodore said.

Margot was pulled out of her daydreaming and shook her head. "I'm sorry. I was gone there for a second."

She grabbed the dice and shook them, then looked at her daughter.

"Give me a six; give me a six."

She rolled the dice onto the table, and they all screamed in excitement as they showed a five and a one.

"Nooo," " Minna complained as Margot took her figure to Times Square and bought it.

Margot chuckled while Minna grabbed a handful of popcorn and threw it at her.

"Why do you always win?"

"I haven't won yet," she said.

"Your mom is right," Theodore said. "We can still get her for this."

"You're always so lucky," Minna said, grumbling. "It doesn't matter what game we play. It's unfair."

"I am hardly that lucky," Margot said, thinking maybe her daughter was right. Maybe she had been lucky once again. She had dodged another bullet with this interview. There wasn't anything that could hurt her now, was there?

"I don't want to play anymore," Minna said, then grabbed the remote and threw herself onto the soft couch. "Let's watch some TV instead."

34

Webster, Florida **1979**

"Another child is missing."

Carol's neighbor, Joel, stared at her. He was standing on her porch, eyes torn in despair, his forehead glistening in sweat.

"It's the Blacks' little boy, Benjamin. He was playing outside in their yard when he disappeared. They can't find him anywhere."

"That's awful," Carol said. "Did they try all of his friends' houses? Did they knock on all the houses on his street and ask if they've seen him?"

Joel nodded and wiped sweat off his forehead with the back of his hand.

"They fear he might have taken off for the swamps. Who knows? He might have seen something…maybe a hog or somethin' and gone after it. He's four years old, for cryin' out loud; there's no saying where he might have run off to."

Carol nodded. That was always the first thing parents feared around here. That their children would run off and drown in the swamps or maybe get pulled underwater by a gator.

"We're creating a search team and thought you might join in?" he asked. "We need as many eyes as possible out there."

Carol looked into the living room where Anna Mae was sitting on the floor, drawing on a piece of paper. She was completely absorbed in her own world. She had been doing well lately, ever since Carol took her in and started homeschooling her. Her grades had gone up a little, and she seemed less aggressive. Earlier in her life, there had been incidents where she had attacked other kids in the schoolyard. One time, she had been sent home after forcing a girl to eat sand; another time, she had tried to strangle a boy who had been bullying her. It was no wonder to Carol that the town didn't like her and that most people feared her. Many still believed she could have killed Timothy. The sheriff had even taken her in for questioning. The attacks on them had died off a little, though, and it had been a while since someone last painted on their garage or smeared their house with eggs. Carol kept the girl at home as much as possible, sensing that was the smart thing to do. But still, she had to let her go outside and play every now and then; she could hardly keep her inside all day. Usually, she went with Bella, and that made Carol feel safe. Anna Mae wouldn't get herself in trouble with Bella around.

Carol sighed, wondering if she should leave the child in the house while she went searching for the Blacks' boy, then decided that maybe people would act nicer to her if they saw her helping out for once.

"We'll be right there," Carol said. "Just give me a second to get ready."

Joel smiled nervously. "We? You're…you plan on bringing Anna Mae too? I thought it would just be you."

"I'm bringing her. She has eyes and ears too, doesn't she?" Carol asked angrily.

"Sure. I just…well…"

"She knows where the kids play around town," Carol interrupted him. "She knows more about where a boy like Ben would be than any of us adults. It would be a shame not to let her help out now, wouldn't it?"

Joel nodded, looking down. "Of course, ma'am."

"Alrighty, then. We'll meet y'all in front of the Blacks' house in a few minutes."

Carol slammed the door shut with a snort. She heard Joel's steps as he walked off the porch. She took in a few deep breaths, trying to gather herself, then smiled wearily at Anna Mae and walked over to her. Anna Mae didn't look up; she was too deep into her drawing. Carol looked down at what she was drawing, then gasped. A tightness in her chest made it hard to breathe, and she felt so dizzy that she had to sit down to regain her composure.

35

I CALLED JULIE AND HAD A LONG CHAT WITH HER. SHE sounded like she had the best day of her life. She and Maggie were back to being best friends again, and it seemed like nothing could throw her off the rails now.

It made me relax a little and relieved some of the huge amount of guilt I was feeling for not coming home yet.

William was his usual happy self when he came to the phone. We talked about the spring concert he was rehearsing for at his pre-school, and he sang a little bit of the ABC-song for me, but then stopped and told me the rest was going to be a surprise, so I'd have to wait.

I hung up, then turned on the TV to watch the local news to relax for a little. I had been staring at my computer for hours, reading through all the old articles, and my head was beginning to hurt. I was wondering what I was still doing here, and why I didn't just go home, but a part of me knew I had to stay. There was something here that I couldn't just turn my back on. Out there somewhere was a killer, and it didn't seem like anyone else cared enough to find him.

The news was filled with stories about furloughed government employees who were hurt by the government shutdown. I dozed off while they changed the subject to a local story about a manatee that had gotten itself stuck in a storm drain.

I woke up with a start a few minutes later. Rubbing my eyes, I sat up straight and stared at the TV, rubbing the cobwebs away from my eyes. A second later, I was fully awake, my eyes big and wide. On the screen in front of me was Joanna. She was standing in front of the old abandoned house, talking to a reporter. Underneath her it read:

BREAKING: FAMOUS AUTHOR REVEALED AS MURDERER

Reporter: "She's not proud of what she is about to say, but this concerned mother feels the need to tell the public about what her own daughter has done."

Joanna: "I can't believe she's back, and no one knows. She lives right outside of town, and no one has the slightest idea."

Reporter: "In the town of Webster, they all remember that fatal morning forty years ago when the body of young Timothy Peterson was found inside this abandoned house. At first, they all believed it was nothing but a terrible accident, until the next child disappeared."

Joanna: "That was when they started to suspect my daughter, but they couldn't prove it. Besides, no one would ever believe that a ten-year-old could have killed a toddler, right? But she did."

Reporter: "Now, this mother claims her murderous daughter is living right outside of town, and no one has even realized it."

Joanna: "I'm telling you…it's her. She has the entire world fooled. Margot Addington, the famous author, is the very same one who killed Timothy Peterson inside this house. And I'm certain she also killed that other kid recently."

Reporter: "You mean Alexander Cunningham?"

Joanna: "Yes. She killed him too."

Reporter: "But the police says that Alexander died in an accident. Why do you say that he was killed?"

Joanna: "They said Timothy's death was an accident too, but I know she killed him. A mother knows these things. She's back, and she's killing again."

Reporter: "So, you claim that Margot Addington is your daughter?"

Joanna: "Yes, she is. I'm not proud of it or what she has done, but she is. I recognized her when I saw that article today in some magazine. She is my Anna Mae, and she was convicted of murdering Timothy Peterson and poor little Benjamin Black back in nineteen seventy-nine. She's changed her name. She's changed the way she looks, but you can't run from who you are. Your momma always knows. I've chosen to come forward to warn our town. Margot Addington is Anna Mae Burke. And she's nothing but a murderer. Keep your children at home. Don't let them run out on their own."

Next, Joanna held up an old photo of a child with a pageboy haircut and stated that this was what she looked like as a child. The reporter then turned to the camera and said:

"Now, we have naturally tried to get a comment from the sheriff's office today, but Sheriff Travers says he has nothing more to add. Alexander Cunningham died in a tragic accident was all he had to say. Back to you, Chad."

As they returned to the studio, I turned the TV off, heart pounding in my chest. I couldn't believe the reporter. She hadn't even tried to contact Margot Addington and ask her for a comment? And where was the proof of any of this? Had they just accepted this crazy woman's explanation because they wanted dirt on a celebrity? I knew that Margot Addington was especially interesting because she had managed to keep her life so private. It was almost as good as if they had caught the Queen shoplifting at Target.

But still. Why would you just let a woman rant on like that without any proof to what she was saying?

It made me so angry. How could they smear Margot Addington's name like this? This was going to hurt her deeply, and they didn't even care, did they?

Sometimes, I loathed my own profession.

I leaned back on the bed, an avalanche of guilt rushing through me. This was all my fault, wasn't it? My article was what led this crazy woman to begin her ranting. I was the reason this had begun, and now the media would throw themselves at it, at Margot. No matter if it was true or not; this was a good story…no, it was a great story. They weren't going to leave Margot alone about this. And to think that she clearly didn't even want to give the interview. All she wanted was to keep to herself and to stay anonymous to the public so she could write her books.

But, what if it's true, Rebekka? What if it is really the same person? Could she have killed Alexander Cunningham?

I shook my head. It was so easy to get carried away like that. I wasn't going to let it happen to me. I had to keep my cool and let the facts talk. Rumors and loose statements weren't enough. I couldn't do what every other journalist around here would over the next couple of days. I had to keep professional about it.

Someone had to.

36

She couldn't breathe. Margot Addington stared at the screen in her living room, feeling like she was suffocating. It was too quiet around her. Both Minna and Theodore stared at the screen, even though Theodore had turned it off. It was so quiet that Margot could hear her own heartbeat.

"Who the heck do they think they are?" Theodore finally said and rose from the couch. The remote in his hand was shaking.

Margot didn't dare to look at him or her daughter. She stared at the carpet beneath her, unable to say a word.

"I mean...why? Why would they run something like that, huh?" he asked. "That woman is obviously crazy as a bat. Anyone can see that. And to claim...to claim that she's your mother...when everyone knows you lost your mother when you were just a child. I can't believe them. Holding out the microphone for anyone these days to say whatever they like. That's not journalism."

Margot felt her daughter's small hand leaning on her arm. "Are you all right, Mom? Are you okay?"

Margot lifted her eyes and looked into those of her daughter. The sight of them made her warm inside. There was no one she loved more in life. She shook her head.

"Oh, Mom," her daughter said and put her head on her shoulder. "I'm sorry. They're just bastards, those journalists. They're trying to hurt you. I'm sure no one will even believe them."

"Why they are even giving that crazy woman any airtime is beyond me," Theodore said. "Can anyone just say anything now and they'll hold out the microphone for her?"

He sat back down with an exhale, rubbing his temples. Minna kept her head on Margot's shoulder.

"It's gonna be okay, Mom," she said. "You don't have to care about what they say. They're nothing but mean bullies."

"I'll call the editor in the morning," Theodore said. "I'll have them run a correction. They can't just spread lies about people and ruin them like this. I will not let it happen. What will your publisher think?"

"I don't think I care much about my publisher right now," Margot said. "I just want to them to leave me alone."

"You should care," he said. "Think about what it might cost you in book sales."

"It's…it's okay, Theodore," she said. "You don't have to…"

He rose to his feet again. "But I want to, and I have to. It's my name too that is being smeared. I will not let them get away with this."

"Please," Margot pleaded. "You'll only make it worse. I just…I should never have done that interview in the first place. That's what started it all."

"So, now it's my fault?" Theodore asked. "Because I

encouraged you to do it? Because I thought it was a good idea?"

Margot shook her head. "No. No, I didn't mean that. I just...I knew it was a terrible idea. Nothing good ever comes from talking to journalists."

"You're darn right," Theodore said. "And from now on, we're not talking to any more of them. Never again. If they write more lies about you, we'll sue them."

Margot looked up, and their eyes met. For just a second, she was certain she saw doubt in his eyes, but then it was gone.

"It's late," he said and turned around. "I'm going to bed."

37

I WENT TO MY CAR FIRST THING THE NEXT MORNING.
Without eating anything, I drove out of town until I
reached Margot Addington's estate. By going early, I had
hoped I would beat everyone else there, but as I drove
closer, it was obvious that I hadn't come early enough.

A huge crowd swarmed the gates. Reporters from
everywhere were set up there. Cameras were ready to snap
a shot of Margot should she appear, and the journalists
held their microphones ready to record her answer if they
got a chance to yell their questions at her, maybe while she
drove out through the gate. Photographers were in the
bushes, their lenses pointed at the estate behind the trees,
looking for just that one shot of her showing up outside. I
sighed and slowed the car down to a stop. I spotted vans
from all the major TV networks. This was a huge story
now and out of my hands.

What have I done?

As I sat there in my car, my phone rang. I picked it up.
It was the editor of the magazine.

"Why the heck didn't you give us this story? Why did I

hear it from somewhere else? Weren't you just with Margot Addington? You had better access to her than any reporter has ever had, and then this story breaks just a few days later?"

I sighed. "I...I didn't know. This came out after I had been at her house."

"It's the biggest story of the year, Rebekka, and you missed it. I don't think it will be easy for you to get work in this business again."

Then she hung up.

I couldn't blame her. I could see how it looked from her point of view. I had to be the worst journalist in the world for not finding this story myself when it was right under my nose. It didn't paint the picture of me as a very thorough journalist. Not in the eyes of an editor who wanted more readers in a world where most magazines were dying a slow death.

I stared at the crowd of journalists who were waiting. I suddenly felt very much like the odd kid out. The last thing I wanted was to be one of them again.

I got out of the car and walked up to them, then elbowed my way through. "Excuse me. Can I just...excuse me?"

I managed to get all the way to the intercom. I could hear the other reporters whispering my name behind me. Guess I had somehow made a name for myself, even though it was in the worst possible way. I was now officially the journalist who had missed the scoop of a lifetime.

I pressed the button, and a voice responded. "Yes?"

It was her. Margot Addington.

"Margot? This is Rebekka Franck. Listen, I..."

"Rebekka Franck? How do you have the nerve to show yourself here?" she said.

My heart sank. Her voice held so much contempt, I could barely stand it. She truly believed this was my fault.

"I'm so sorry, Margot. I never meant for…"

"Haven't you done enough?" she asked. "Please, just leave us alone and take all your little friends with you."

"But…I'm sorry, Margot," I tried. "I had no idea it would end like this."

"We have nothing more to say to one another. Goodbye."

"But…Margot…I…"

It was too late for my apologies. Margot was no longer at the other end. I felt so devastated. This was never my intention. How was I supposed to know this would happen? I wanted to tell her how sorry I was; I wanted to offer to publish her real story instead, to correct it and clear her name, but I didn't even get to say the words.

Instead, I turned around, and that was when all the cameras were turned in my direction. Microphones were held out, and the cameras whirred. All eyes were suddenly lingering on me.

"You've been to her house," a reporter said. "You've interviewed her. Is it true that she is a convicted murderer?"

"Did she kill those boys?" another one yelled.

"Has she killed again?"

"You really are vultures, aren't you?" I answered, then turned around and walked away. A couple of them followed me, yelling more questions at me as I rushed back to my car, feeling so embarrassed about my own profession that I wanted to throw up.

38

It was getting worse. The Blacks' boy hadn't shown up yet, and for two whole days, the town was turned upside down. Everything stopped. No stores were open; no one went to work. Everyone was searching for him, desperately going through every corner of town and every part of the swamps. Still, there was no trace of him, and now everyone had turned their eyes toward Carol's house and the little girl living inside it.

Carol watched as they threw eggs at the façade and yelled for Anna Mae to come out and admit to what she had done. Meanwhile, Carol stared at the drawing that Anna Mae had made two days ago, holding it between her hands, her fingers shaking. It showed a little boy lying in water, his eyes closed.

Ever since Carol had seen the drawing, she had locked the door, and they hadn't left the house. She didn't dare to go out because she felt terrified and had no idea what to do.

She didn't even dare ask the girl about the drawing.

She knew she had to at some point, but she didn't want to. She didn't want to hear the answer. She feared what the girl might say.

Carol loved having Anna Mae in her house and having her with her. Even though John wasn't as pleased about it as she was. She would do anything for the girl. She was her one and only love.

But lately, the girl had begun to frighten her a little. A week ago, she had come to their room at night. She hadn't said anything; they simply woke up to her standing at the end of their bed. It gave Carol a shock, and it took a few seconds before she could get herself together.

"Anna Mae, dear?" Carol asked.

When the girl didn't answer, Carol believed her to be simply sleepwalking. She got out of bed and grabbed Anna Mae's hand. She had then led her back to her bed and tucked her in. But that was when the girl had said something that back then Carol hadn't worried about, but now she did.

"It's more fun to hurt someone who doesn't fight back."

Back then, Carol had thought she was talking about herself, about the kids bullying her in school, but now as she stared at the drawing of the boy, lying in the water, she felt more and more like it held another meaning.

Carol folded the drawing, and with determined steps, she walked out to the backyard where Anna Mae was kneeling on the ground, roasting ants with a magnifying glass. Carol stood behind her for a few seconds, gathering the courage she needed for this.

"Anna Mae?"

The girl looked up, an eerie grin on her face. Carol held out the drawing for her, trying to keep her hands still. Then she pointed at it.

"I need you to take me there. Take me to that place."

The girl's face froze. Anna Mae rose to her feet, then looked at the drawing. She glanced back up at Carol, who realized that even her eyes seemed to be glistening in excitement.

"I'll take you there. Come."

39

She shouldn't have come. Margot felt the many eyes on her as she walked inside with Theodore, her long dress sliding across the marble floor behind her.

She had told him she didn't want to go, but he had insisted that they go. This charity was the event of the year, and they were expected to show up. Besides, if they didn't, then the vultures would win.

Those were his words, and they still rang in her head as she slid across the floor, her high heels clicking on the tiles. There had been chatting and even laughter when she entered, but that all stopped now. Eyes lingered on her, looking at her dress, wondering if it was true, if what they said on TV and online could be real.

They had to take the back entrance out of their house and the estate since the front was still occupied by the journalists. Margot wondered how long they would be camping out there in front of their gate. It was dark when she and Theodore left the comfort of their estate for this dinner, but there were still as many out there as there had been this morning.

Were they never going to give up? Would they never go home? Was this nightmare ever going to end?

"Just breathe," Theodore whispered in her ear, holding her hand in his. "Long, deep breaths. I promise it'll all be over soon."

Margot tried. She tried to breathe and smile at the same time. She tried so hard to pretend like everything was just fine when all she wanted was to scream. She wanted to go home and just stay there forever behind those closed doors where no one could see her or judge her. She wanted never to show her face anywhere again.

They had followed them to the event. Two cars with journalists and photographers in them had seen them leave through the back entrance and followed them there. They had driven up on the side of the car and yelled out the window, trying to get any reaction out of her or her husband, anything they could get a picture of that they could sell. She had heard the clicking of cameras as she rushed inside the Ritz-Carlton in Orlando, Theodore trying to cover her up so they couldn't take her picture.

Her husband did his best, but he couldn't protect her against what had met them on the inside. People who used to be their friends were staring her down, their eyes oozing with condemnation. Even the lady showing them to their table gave her one of those looks that told her she was worthless; she was the scum of the Earth.

"Can we go home soon?" she whispered as the event went on and she felt like she had shown her face for long enough. "I really want to go home."

Theodore grabbed her hand in his and rubbed it gently. "Soon. Let's just stay a little while longer to make sure that people know you won't scare away easily. You have every bit as much right to be here as they have. You're doing fine; trust me."

Margot leaned back in the chair and sipped her wine. As the soft drops touched her tongue, she kept going, and soon she had emptied her glass. She closed her eyes and let the drink do its job in her, letting the divine drops of heaven subdue her raging fear. The waiter then filled her glass again, and she soon finished that one as well.

"Let's go," Theodore finally said when the event was almost over. "I think that ought to do it. If we go now, we can make it out to the car before everyone else. That should give us a head start."

Margot rose to her feet and staggered toward the entrance, holding the hand of her beloved husband. They reached the door, and he held it open for her, so she could walk ahead. Margot walked outside, feeling woozy but thankful that it was all over, and she could finally go back home.

As Theodore closed the door behind her, she spotted the crowd of journalists. When they saw her, they bounced forward, all of them simultaneously yelling her name.

Margot froze as they approached with their clicking cameras. But it was no longer them she was seeing.

It was the small woman in ragged clothes standing in front of them that had caught her eye. The woman had gotten old. The eyes were older, yet the same. They had the same spite in them as they'd had earlier in Margot's life.

"Well, well, well," the woman simply said. "How you have made your way up in this world, my Anna Mae."

Margot stared at the woman, her heart thumping in her chest. She tried to walk around the woman, still holding her husband's arm, but the woman wouldn't let them pass.

"You think you've fooled the entire world, don't you?

But not me, Anna Mae. You'll never fool me. I know who you really are."

"Leave me alone," Margot said. "I don't know who you are. Get away from me."

That made the woman laugh. "You don't know who I am. Now that is one for the books. My own daughter doesn't even recognize me."

The cameras were flashing as the words fell like rocks from the sky. Margot felt her legs begin to shake and knew she had to act. She had to get away from here now before her entire world crumbled.

"Please, leave us alone," Theodore said. He was speaking politely, yet with the authority of a doctor.

"You even have him fooled, don't you?" the woman said.

Theodore shook his head in contempt, and she could tell he was about to get agitated. This was beneath him. He wasn't used to humiliation; he wasn't used to people talking to him without an air of awe and respect.

"Listen to me," he began. "I don't know who you are or why you believe you can just come here…"

But he didn't make it any further before the woman walked closer and looked him straight in his eyes. Behind them, the cameras were flashing like a lightning storm. The reporters were watching it all, gobbling it down, mouths gaping, and drooling over the story they were about to get, probably already making up sensational headlines in their minds.

"No, you listen to me," the woman said. "Your wife is my daughter. I would recognize those eyes anywhere. And she's a murderer. You ask her about that when you get home. And ask her about the scar she has on the lower part of her back. Because I gave it to her when she was seven, trying to kill her with a fire poker. You ask her about that, and then you tell me who is lying."

"I don't have to listen to this," Theodore said, shaking his head. "Please, just leave my wife alone."

Margot felt his hand on her arm, and she was pulled away. His determined footsteps walked across the pavement to the car that the parking valet had ready for them. There was something more to those steps now, wasn't there? There was an anger in them that she hadn't heard before.

Margot got into the car, and they rushed off, the engine roaring, while the cameras flashed and the reporters yelled, trying to suck out the last of what was left of the famous and mysterious Margot Addington.

40

I saw it on Facebook. I had decided to boycott the TV and went on Facebook for just a few seconds when it popped up in my feed. A live broadcast from some charity event in Orlando. I watched as Margot Addington faced the woman who claimed to be her mother. I saw Joanna once again claim she knew who she really was. I couldn't believe what was happening to her. I felt so disgusted with the entire situation and could tell how terrible it made Margot feel. But they didn't care. All they wanted was some reaction from the woman everyone talked about these days. They just trusted this strange woman who suddenly made all these claims.

Was this what things had come to now? Was this what they called journalism now? Was it all about destroying people's lives to get clicks and sell magazines? I remembered a day when it was all about the truth and finding it. That's what it was like when I chose to get into journalism. That was what it was all about when I was in Afghanistan and when I took down corrupt politicians.

I missed those days.

What if they're right, Rebekka? What if she is Anna Mae Burke? What if she did kill Alexander Cunningham?

I shook my head to get rid of the thought. There was no evidence that connected Margot to the boy, and until there was, I chose to believe she was innocent. I wasn't going to let some lynch mob dictate what I believed. I needed proof, and I needed facts.

I hadn't gotten anywhere on the case all day, but in all fairness, I hadn't been able to concentrate either. I had been so angry and felt so terrible for Margot. I had really liked her when I met her, and I couldn't understand why they were so busy smearing her.

I also felt like I ought to somehow make it up to her, and that's what I was trying to do. I wanted to figure out what the heck was going on in this strange town. Why was the sheriff lying to the parents and the public about Alexander's death? Was it just because he didn't want a repeat of what had happened back in seventy-nine? Did he know more than he let on? I had looked him up and realized he was a young deputy back then. He had been one of the deputies on the scene when they found the Blacks' boy. Maybe he had a personal reason for lying?

I shook my head and closed my computer, feeling awful for Margot. They were so busy calling her a liar and asking themselves if she might have killed again. The worst part was that there wasn't much I could do about what was happening to her, except try and find the truth in this story. It was out there somewhere; I just had to dig a little deeper.

But that also meant I had to stay in this town longer. I wasn't sure my children were too happy about that, not to mention Sune.

I stared at my phone, thinking about him and how much I missed him. He used to be with me on stories like these, and we would figure the truth out together, by digging and digging till it could hide no longer. The thought made me feel more alone than ever, and I let it go. I was done with him. There was no doubt. I had lost all my feelings for him when I walked in on him kissing that nurse. He could make all the excuses he wanted to, but I was done; it was over. I just missed him, that's all, and I wondered if I would ever stop doing that.

41

He still wasn't talking to her. Theodore hadn't said a word to her on the drive home, nor had he made a sound since they walked inside the house. Margot stood by the window and stared into the darkness. The lightness she had felt from drinking the wine earlier was gone, and there was nothing but heavy thoughts left in her mind.

Theodore sat in his Herman Miller lounge chair in the living room. Every now and then, a small moan would emerge from his throat, but that was all that told her he was still there.

Please, say something. Talk to me.

Margot didn't understand what he was waiting for, why he was just sitting there. She had expected him to yell at her, to scold her and ask for an explanation, but so far, he hadn't. Was he waiting for her to break the silence?

It was the scar that had changed everything. The fact that the woman had known about it…since it was located too far down for anyone to be able to see or know about it other than by seeing Margot naked. There was no way

Margot could explain herself out of this one. Did he expect her to at least try? Or was it all lost?

She wanted him to tell her it was okay, that he loved her no matter what. That's what she was waiting for. They had been married for fifteen years. Didn't that count for anything?

"You lied to me, didn't you? For all this time, you've lied to me?" he said from the darkness behind her, finally breaking the silence.

Margot closed her eyes. She didn't turn around to look at him. She weighed her words with cautiousness. It was important how they were put now; she had to be careful with exactly what she said and how she said it. One wrong word could make this situation worse. She still believed she had a chance to save this. She desperately hoped she did.

She decided honesty was the way to go. She couldn't lie anymore. She needed to speak the truth.

"I…I'm sorry."

"Why? Why would you lie to me like that?"

She bent her head. "Would you have married me had you known the truth?"

"So, it is true?" he asked. She could detect the contempt in his voice that she had heard so many times before. It was poisonous, dripping with disdain, like it was whispering: *you're worthless, you don't deserve my love.*

Theodore's fist slammed into the table next to him. Margot jumped at the sound.

"Answer me. Is it TRUE?"

She swallowed. For a painful moment, all she could hear was his heavy, agitated breathing.

Then she nodded.

He rose to his feet. "So, you're a killer? You're a murderer?"

The words felt like knives to her body. They cut through her, leaving nothing but pain.

He groaned loudly. She wanted to turn around and beg him to forgive her, to just let it go, plead with him to remember the love they had shared, the child they had together, and ask him, what did it matter? She was still the same. Nothing had changed on her part.

But she didn't. She didn't dare to. She knew what she was, and she knew running from it had been a mistake. But it was too late now; there was no going back. What was done was done.

"I'm going to bed," he said. "I'll be gone in the morning. You can keep the house, but I won't be living here. I'll make sure you and Minna are taken care of."

Hearing this, she turned with a gasp and met his dark eyes across the room. He lifted his nose and looked down at her like she was unworthy of his presence.

"I don't care about money," she said. "All I care about is you. Don't you understand? I love you. Being with you was never about the money. I don't want to live without you. I don't think I can go on without you in my life. What am I supposed to do?"

She said the words, even though she knew they were wasted. There was nothing more she could do. It was over.

Theodore gave her one last glance, then turned around and walked up the stairs toward their bedroom. Margot stared after him even long after he was gone. Her mouth was open in a soundless scream, her body shaking, and she hugged herself while everything screamed inside of her. For so many years, she had tried to escape her past. She had changed her name, she had changed the way she looked, but it still caught up to her.

Margot rushed to the top drawer and pulled out a pack of cigarettes. She hadn't smoked in years, but for some reason, she had kept the package. She pulled one out and lit it, then inhaled sharply and closed her eyes. She sat down by the dinner table, her body feeling like it was made of lead. Her hand shook as she directed the cigarette toward her lips again and took in another deep inhale. Tears ran across her cheeks while she blew out a cloud of smoke.

I'll be gone in the morning.

He had said the words like it was the simplest thing in the world, to just up and leave her. Like it was so easy.

Margot smoked again and felt the warm air as it reached her lungs. It was Theodore who had made her stop back in the day because smoking would kill her one day.

"What irony," she whispered and blew out another cloud.

As the burning cigarette caught onto the curtains and flames licked the walls downstairs, Margot got dressed for the night upstairs. When she laid down in the bed next to Theodore and pulled the covers over her freezing body, she could already feel the warmth rising from the floor below them.

Smoke hit her nostrils and soon made it hard to breathe. Margot closed her eyes, feeling at peace for the first time in her long and painful life.

Finally. It ends here.

42

I couldn't sleep. It would be an understatement to say that a thousand thoughts rushed through my mind. I couldn't find rest at all and kept pacing around in my room, asking myself what to do next. Should I go back home? It would be the sensible thing to do, to just let it go. But how could I leave with everything that I knew?

I had a terrible headache on top of it all and realized there was no way I could fall asleep with this pounding feeling behind my eyes. I had to find some ibuprofen somewhere.

I got dressed and then walked down to the lobby where Adeline's daughter, Regina, sat in the back, reading a book. She often took the nightshift for her older mother.

"Excuse me?" I asked. "Hello?"

Regina stuck her head out of the back room. "Yes? Hi there. Can I help you?"

"Do you have any ibuprofen or Advil lying around? I have a terrible headache."

Regina smiled. "Sure. We always keep some for guests. Let me just find it for you."

She got up, and I could hear her rummaging around in the back before she returned.

"I'm sorry. We usually always have some, but I'm afraid that we seem to have run out."

"Just my luck," I said with a scoff. "How far is the nearest 24-hour pharmacy?"

Her face looked torn. "That'll be about a fifteen-minute drive from here, in Bushnell."

I looked at the clock. It was almost midnight. I sighed, thinking that if I hurried, I could still make it back here by one and get a few hours of good sleep. I didn't have to get up early anyway.

"I'm sorry," Regina added. "Like I said, we usually have some in the back."

I smiled. It wasn't her fault. "Just not today. Don't worry about it. I'll do the drive. I have to have something for this terrible headache if I plan on sleeping at all tonight."

I thanked Regina for trying, then walked back to my room and grabbed the car keys and my phone. I drove off into the clear night, thinking this little drive might end up doing me good. I would most definitely be exhausted once I got back.

I turned up the radio and sang along to Adele while driving out of town, pleased to see that there wasn't a car on the road ahead. It was just me and Adele rushing through the darkness, singing about our broken hearts, reminding me how Sune and I *almost had it all* and how much I missed being a family.

After singing along for a little while, I changed the station. Not because I didn't love Adele but because the song reminded me of how terrible my life was right now, and it overwhelmed me. It stirred me up a little more than I cared for. Next, Carrie Underwood blasted out of my speakers, singing about how her man was putting his moves on some Shania wannabe with no taste for whiskey. I sang along while thinking about how I had felt at first when I had found Sune with that woman. My first reaction had been anger. I had yelled at him, saying the most hurtful things. I wanted to hurt him for what he had done to us; I wanted him to feel what I felt. I wanted him to be in as much pain as I was, but no matter how much I tried to hurt him, it didn't make my pain go away. I don't know why I thought it would.

I drove for about ten minutes, letting my phone's GPS guide me toward the pharmacy that was located in the neighboring town of Bushnell. The countryside was very dark at night, and I felt like I was in one of those horror movies when you just waited for something to show up in the headlights of the car.

And something did show up. Not in my headlights, but it did strike me with great horror. As I took a turn and drove down a big road, I saw flames. Flames licking the sky, lighting up the darkness. As I drove closer, I realized with terror where they came from.

Margot!

43

"Oh, dear God!"

I stopped the car by the gate, then got out. The flames stood tall between the trees, and I knew they had to come from the main house. The horses were screaming in the night.

I grabbed my phone, then dialed 911. A few anxious minutes later, the fire truck arrived, sirens wailing. A firefighter rolled the window down briefly, and I told him I was the one who had called.

"I think there are still people in the house, but I can't get through the gate," I said.

"We'll take it from here," he said.

Next, they drove through the gate. They simply just slammed the firetruck through it, and the gate crumpled when meeting this mighty vehicle with all its heavy weight. After that one, another fire truck joined it, and they rushed by, while I prayed that Margot and her family were all right.

I drove up the trail after the trucks had gone by, then

stopped the car at a safe distance. I got out, heart throbbing in my chest. The warmth from the fire felt like it was burning my face. I was devastated. Their car was in the driveway. Were they still in there somewhere?

Please, let them be out of town. Let them be somewhere else.

As I finished the thought and pushed away the terror it filled me with, a firefighter came out of the burning building, walking through the flames, carrying someone in his arms. My heart stood still while he placed the child in the arms of someone else.

"There are more; I'm going back in," he yelled, right before he turned around and went back inside.

In the distance, I could hear more sirens and guessed the police were coming now too and hopefully an ambulance. I held my breath as I watched the entrance to the house, waiting for the firefighter to reappear, hopefully carrying someone else out. The flames were close to the roof now, and even though they blasted water on it, it didn't seem to do much. As soon as they gained control of one area, another exploded and took over.

It's taking too long. Why is it taking so long?

The firefighters yelled as the ambulance drove up the trail, sirens blaring loudly. I stared, completely paralyzed, at the entrance to the house where the firefighter from earlier once again came out, this time carrying Margot's husband, Theodore Addington. To my surprise, he wasn't alone. Another firefighter came up behind him, carrying a lifeless Margot Addington in his arms.

The paramedics threw themselves at all three while the flames took complete control of the building. It soon became obvious that there wasn't much to do to save it. All the firefighters could do now was to make sure it didn't spread to the stables. They had let the horses out and let them run into the field. Meanwhile, Margot and her family were all taken into the ambulances and rushed away.

I watched them leave, my heart aching badly, praying that they would all make it.

44

WEBSTER, FLORIDA 1979

Carol followed Anna Mae through town. Much to her surprise, it seemed almost like Anna Mae was enjoying this little trip they were on like it was some adventure.

Was it all a game to her?

Meanwhile, Carol felt terrified beyond compare. What if she was right? What if the girl really led her to the Blacks' boy? What would she do?

Carol bit her nails as she followed the girl across the railroad tracks, through a junkyard, and closer to the swamps. It was late in the day, and the sun would set in about an hour or so. It was a time when most townsfolk would be at home eating dinner. That was why Carol had chosen this hour, to minimize the risk of being seen.

"Will we be there soon?" she asked, her voice trembling. "Anna Mae? Are we getting closer?"

The girl nodded. "We're almost there. Just a few more minutes."

"Okay, maybe we should hurry up then," Carol said and glanced toward the tall trees where the sun would be setting soon. She didn't want to be anywhere near the swamps when it got dark.

Anna Mae sped up, and Carol followed her. They rushed through a small field of grass in a vacant lot when Anna Mae turned around and looked at Carol, then signaled for her to follow her closely.

The lot was overgrown and almost impassable, but Anna Mae knew how to get through the thick vegetation. Soon, they were standing in between the many trees, and Anna Mae pointed.

"Over there. Down in that hole."

Anna Mae walked ahead of Carol and knelt next to what appeared to be barely more than a hole in the ground. It had a ring of rocks around it, but it was hard to see unless you came up really close. Carol knelt next to Anna Mae, then peeked inside the deep hole. Water was gurgling beneath her, and that was when she realized it was an abandoned well that had never been sealed off properly.

She gasped and looked quickly at Anna Mae, then shone the flashlight she had brought in case they were caught outside once the sun had gone down. The beam of light landed on something in the water, and it made Carol want to throw up.

Benjamin Black.

Carol gasped and pulled back. She looked at Anna Mae, then grabbed her by the shoulders.

"What have you done to him? Anna Mae? Tell me what you did to the poor boy!"

Anna Mae shook her head. "No. No, Aunt Carol. He fell. He fell into the hole."

"Don't you dare lie to me," Carol said and slapped her cheek. Her lips were quivering. She felt so frightened. Had she harbored a killer in her house? Was everyone right about her?

Anna Mae felt her cheek where Carol's fingers had hit, and her eyes changed drastically. Her nostrils flared, and she took a step backward, still holding her cheek.

"Anna Mae, tell me the truth," Carol almost yelled. "Tell me the truth, now!"

Anna Mae backed up further while her eyes grew darker and darker. Then, the girl turned around and took off running, sliding through the bushes faster than Carol could grab her.

"Come back here, Anna Mae! You hear me, Anna Mae? Anna Mae?"

45

She didn't even look at me when I entered her room at the hospital. I felt a lump in my throat as I knocked gently on the already open door, then walked inside.

"M-Margot?"

In my hand, I had a bouquet of flowers, but they made me feel so silly, and I placed them on a table without giving them to her. Flowers were probably the last thing she needed right now after having survived both her husband and daughter.

I felt tears press behind my eyes, and it was hard to keep them at bay. I walked closer while she continued to stare out the window. The nurse told me that she had been like that all day since she received the news of her family's death. She also told me they were very happy to see a visitor since Margot hadn't given them any relatives to contact. Luckily, the media had found some other story to chase. Apparently, some tennis player out west had slept with her best friend's husband and gotten themselves in some car accident where said tennis player had been drunk. Now, they were throwing themselves at that instead and leaving Margot alone.

They had chewed her up and spat her out again. This was all there was left of her, and now she was alone in the world.

"I...I am so sorry," I said. "You can't imagine how terrible I feel."

Margot still stared out the window, not even acknowledging my presence. She was barely moving in her bed. Only her chest was heaving up and down as she breathed.

"Just...leave," she said in almost a whisper.

"I'm not sure I can do that," I said, then cleared my throat. "I've read up on your story, and the story of Anna Mae Burke. I know you want me to leave it alone, but I don't think I can..."

Margot closed her eyes. "I did my time."

I stared at her, not knowing what to say. This had been following her all her life. She had been imprisoned at only ten years old, in a prison with adults, doing things to her one could only imagine. It had to have been a true nightmare. And then when she got out, twenty years later, she had changed her name and tried to start over. She had started to write books and met a man whom she had a child with. She had believed her life was on the right track, that she had been able to put the past behind her. She had made a life for herself, but it caught up to her in the end. She was never going to escape it, was she?

"Did you kill those two kids?" I asked. I knew it was bold; I knew it might upset her, but I had to know. "You claimed your innocence till the end but were convicted by a unanimous jury. Were you innocent?"

Finally, Margot turned her head and looked directly at me. Her usually so sparkling blue eyes had grown matte and lifeless. Half a smile slid across her face.

"What does it matter? You know the prisons are filled with people claiming to be innocent, right? What do you even care? You have a life. You have your family. Why don't you go back to them and leave me alone? I have nothing left. Nothing!"

"But surely, you must have some…"

She lifted her hand to stop me. "Just leave, will you?"

Her eyes drifted once again toward the window, and I could tell it was my cue to go. I turned around and walked to the door, then paused. I glanced once more back at her. I felt compelled to tell her how sorry I felt for everything, but I didn't.

Instead, I left, phone clutched tightly in my hand, calling Julie.

46

"Do you have anyone we can call to come and get you? Any family or friends maybe?"

The nurse stood in the doorway while Margot sat on the edge of the bed. The doctor had just done his rounds and told her she would be discharged. Her daughter had died from burns to her respiratory system, while her husband had suffered a heart attack from lack of oxygen because of smoke inhalation. Meanwhile, Margot seemed to be perfectly fine. They had kept her for two days for observation for smoke inhalation and taken care of the burns on her arms and legs. Now, they had told her she was ready to go home.

"Home?" she had asked. "Where is that?"

To that, the doctor had answered with merely a shrug, then left. They had given her a set of clothes that some other patient had left behind, and she had put them on. The pants were big, and she had to hold onto them to not lose them when she walked.

"I'm good; I don't need to be picked up," Margot told

the nurse, then rose to her feet in the shoes that were two sizes too big.

"Are you sure? A traumatic experience like this, it might be good to have someone to share it with…"

Margot walked up to her and looked her in the eyes. "I'll be fine. I don't need anyone. Not anymore."

Then she left. With her head held as high as she could, hiding her devastation on the inside the way life had taught her to, Margot walked into the elevator, pushed the button, and let it take her down to the lobby. Outside, she stopped a taxi and let it take her back to her estate, or what was left of it.

Luckily, Theodore always kept cash in the car, and since it was still parked outside, unlocked, she could grab some to pay the taxi driver. Much to her surprise, she found both money and one of Theodore's credit cards. He had also left the keys to the car in the glove compartment like he often did because he didn't want to have to search for his keys in the mornings when he had to rush off. But that meant she had a car and a credit card she could use to go and buy some new clothes and food.

There was a house behind the stables that was used to house the caretaker of the horses. There was even a small bed in there where she could sleep. The caretaker didn't need to come anymore since she would take care of the horses herself from now on. They were all she had left.

Margot stared after the taxi as it disappeared down the road, then turned to look at what was left of her house, of her entire life. Her once so beautiful house that had once contained so much joy, so much love.

It was all gone.

The horses whinnied. They were still running in the field and had probably already forgotten everything that had taken place just a few nights before.

Oh, to be a horse, she thought to herself. *To be able to let go of the past and the pain just like that. It must be heaven.*

Margot approached the ruins of her life, then reached down and touched a wooden beam that had fallen and blocked the entrance. She pushed it aside, then walked into the empty ruins, looking around to see if there was anything she could save.

The roof was gone. Most of the walls were still standing but had turned black with soot. Her metal patio furniture was still on the porch, or what was left of it. Margot grabbed a chair and sat on it, then stared at the remains of her house.

She looked up at the sky above her, then wondered why God had let her live. Instead of dying with the others, Margot had survived and was now left completely alone.

Was God really that cruel? Did He hate her that much?

47

I CRIED HELPLESSLY FOR ALMOST AN ENTIRE DAY. I DIDN'T know what to do. I wanted to help Margot, but she refused my help. I couldn't bear what had happened to her. It felt so unfair, so unbelievably cruel. I stayed inside my motel room, pacing back and forth, then called my dad back in Denmark and told him the entire story.

"Maybe you can only do so much, Rebekka. It can't be all your fault. You only did an interview. There is no way you could have foreseen what would happen, what chain of events would unfold afterward," he said. "It was unfortunate, yes, but I find it hard to see how it could be your fault."

"But if I hadn't done the stupid interview in the first place, then her mother would never have found out about her, and she would never have revealed her," I said.

"How were you supposed to know? You can't control what people do, Rebekka. There will always be heartbreak; there will always be crazy mothers hurting their children. It happens. That doesn't mean it's your fault, you hear me?"

I sighed. He made me feel slightly better, but I still

couldn't escape the thought that all of this had happened because of me, because of my article. I didn't even want to do it; I just wanted to make some money to make sure my family had a roof over their heads.

"Maybe you should just go home, Rebekka. I'm sure the kids miss you and Sune is in way over his head. Drop the story and let it go. You don't have to write it. You can always find another one."

I nodded, realizing he was right. I had spent so much time in this place, and nothing good had come of it. I wasn't even close to cracking the story open. My children needed me, and to be honest, I needed them just as much.

"I think I will go home now. Tomorrow that is. It's late now. How are you feeling, Dad?"

"I'm actually doing pretty well," he said. "Haven't felt this well in a long time, I might add."

I wondered if he was lying to make me feel better. I had made sure he had a nurse who came to his house several times a day to make sure he ate and got out of bed. I usually kept in touch with her, but lately, I hadn't been calling her much. Not since all this trouble began with Sune.

"That's good to hear. I'm really glad you're better, Dad," I said, choosing to believe him. He sounded well and even slightly happy. It made my heart ache. I missed him so much, but there wasn't really any prospect of me getting to see him anytime soon. I had promised myself I would go home in the summer, hopefully bringing the kids, but that was so far away. It was torture for him to be without us like this, especially since we used to live with him. He never complained, though. That wasn't exactly my dad's style. He always saw the positive in any situation and tried to make the best of what he had.

"I miss you," I said and held the phone closer to my ear. "I miss you so much, and I wish you were here."

"I miss you too," he said. "Now, take good care of yourself and your family, okay? Promise me that."

We hung up, and I sat for a while, staring at the display of my phone. I had received a text from Julie, who once again asked me when I was coming home, then added:

WILLIAM IS DRIVING US ALL CRAZY.

I chuckled, knowing my son could be a little much to handle sometimes. I wondered how Sune's girlfriend dealt with suddenly having three kids to handle that weren't her own. It couldn't be easy.

I AM PACKING UP NOW, I wrote back. COMING HOME TOMORROW.

48

ALLAN CUNNINGHAM LOOKED AT HIS OWN REFLECTION IN the mirror after finishing shaving. He touched his neck and cheek gently, thinking he wasn't doing too terribly for a ninety-two-year-old. He was still living in his own home, even though he had moved into something smaller when his daughter took over the cucumber farm. His wife was dead—four years to the day now—and losing her had made him feel ten years older. Other than that, he was doing pretty well, he thought. He had outlived everyone else, all his siblings and every other relative. He had even outlived his best friends and was now the oldest man in town.

He had lost his vision in one eye but did fine with the one he had left. He was still an avid reader and read both the local paper and the *Wall Street Journal* from cover to cover every day. He enjoyed keeping up with the news of the world and could still win any political debate, should one occur. It wasn't often that Allan was invited out anymore, but his daughter would have him over for dinner at the farm every now and then, and sometimes Allan and her dimwit of a husband, Mark, would engage in a discussion of current affairs. Allan had always believed that his son-in-law was an idiot—and a Democrat on top of it all—and it was no secret that Allan was quite reluctant to let him and his daughter take over the cucumber farm. But Anna, Allan's wife for almost sixty years, had wanted it to be this way. Allan had believed he could run the place until he died, but she didn't want that for them. She wanted to be able to enjoy retirement; she wanted to read books and travel, she said. Allan had told her she could still do all those things, but Anna had given him a look, then said, she wanted to do them with her husband, not alone. Anna had bugged him about it for almost ten years before he gave in. Now, his daughter and that fool were running the place alone. And they were running it into the ground if you asked Allan. He had tried to tell them how it was done, he had tried to give them advice but little did it help. They had taken out loans, and that was going to end up killing the place. If there was one thing Alan had always known, it was you never ever took out a loan from the bank. The bank would own you for the rest of your life, and they could take you down if they wanted to. No, you bought everything cash, and if you didn't have the money, you waited till you did. That was the right way to do business, and that was the way the Cunningham farm had always been run, but oh, no, not anymore. His daughter and her idiot husband had said it wasn't like that anymore in that condescending way they always spoke to him these days like he was a child who needed to have it explained. The cucumber business was changing, they said. It wasn't as lucrative as it had been. There was lots of competition now, and they needed to expand if they were to survive. And in order to expand, they needed money.

"Fools," Allan spat out as he dried off his face with a

towel. He shook his head, wondering if this would be the end of the family business. Since his grandchild Alexander had died, there was no one left to take over after them. If there would even be anything left once they were done.

Allan exhaled, then walked into the kitchen. He had been fishing all day since early in the morning with his fishing buddies out in the swamps, and he'd caught a big red snapper. It was on the counter now, ready to be gutted. Allan was looking forward to that since the gutting was Allan's favorite part. He liked the sound the knife made as it cut into the flesh of the animal. He liked the feeling of slicing through the meat.

As he approached the big fish, he looked for his gutting knife, but it wasn't there. Allan shook his head. He was so certain he had put it out on the counter right after he came home. The plan had been to shower, shave, and then he wanted to prepare the fish and cook it for dinner. He had put the knife on the counter, right there, so it was ready.

Hadn't he?

Oh, you old fool. You can't remember anything these days.

It was true. The day before, when going to Wal-Mart, he had forgotten where he parked the car, and the day before that, he hadn't been able to recall his phone number. His own darn number!

It was normal at his age, he guessed, but it was still annoying as heck.

"Maybe it's in the drawer," he said and pulled it open, but it wasn't there either. Annoyed, he stared at the big fish. Could he have placed the knife somewhere else without knowing it? Maybe in the garage when he got home? Maybe he dropped it in the car?

Confused, Allan was about to turn around to retrace his steps but stopped himself as he heard footsteps coming up behind him. Someone was in the room with him, standing right behind him.

"Looking for this?" a voice said as something cold was pressed against his newly-shaved throat.

Allan didn't have to see it to know it was his gutting knife. He didn't have to turn around and look to know who was holding it either.

"I know why you're here," he said.

"Good. That saves me the time to explain."

Allan opened his mouth to speak, but as he did, the knife penetrated the skin on his throat, and nothing but gurgling sounds escaped his mouth. As he sank to the floor and the light abandoned his eyes, he wondered if it was an angel or the devil he saw before him.

49

WEBSTER, FLORIDA 1979

Carol showed the sheriff through the bushes and guided him to the boy in the well. He had brought all his deputies with him when he heard who she had found. The sheriff went down on his knees and looked inside the hole in the ground. He spotted the boy, then exhaled deeply.

"Oh, my God."

One of his deputies, Travers, volunteered to climb inside the dark well and put a rope around the boy's small body. It took four of them to pull the boy up of the black hole, and soon Benjamin Black was carefully placed in the high grass next to the well.

Carol stared at the pale body while the sheriff took off his hat and held it between his hands, tears springing to his eyes.

"Oh, dear Lord," he mumbled.

Deputy Travers climbed up from inside the well and walked to the small body, sobbing loudly, unable to keep it back anymore. Carol knew he was best friends with the boy's father, Steven Black. They had grown up together, and the Blacks had made Deputy Travers the godfather of Benjamin when he was born. He was known to have played ball with Benjamin whenever he got the chance and had taken the boy fishing at least once a month.

Deputy Travers knelt next to the boy, covering his mouth with his hand, crying, but trying to hold it back.

"What have they done to him?" he said and finally broke down completely. His entire body was trembling as he cried, hovering over the boy. It was tough for Carol to watch and not cry herself. The sheriff walked closer and placed a hand on Travers' shoulder for comfort, and no one spoke for a long time. Carol felt like she had to throw up.

Dear God, Anna Mae. Did you do this? Did you?

Carol still found it hard to believe. After all, Anna Mae was nothing but a child. Strange, yes, but still. How could a child be capable of committing such an atrocity? It didn't seem possible.

"What's that?" another deputy asked, then pointed at the young boy's right arm. "What's that on his arm?"

The sheriff bent over him and took a closer look. Carol approached too. She almost didn't dare to, but still, she looked down. What she saw made her body shake in despair.

"It looks like someone carved something into his arm, doesn't it?" the deputy asked.

"What is it?" another deputy asked.

The sheriff paused, then ran a finger across it, removing dirt. "It looks like a letter. It looks like the letter A."

As he said the last part, he lifted his gaze and looked at Carol. Carol felt so sick that she tasted bile in the back of her mouth. She groaned so she wouldn't throw up and turned her head away. The sheriff looked at her, then rose to his feet, putting his hat back on. He gave Carol a stern look.

"I'm afraid we need to have a very serious talk with Anna Mae."

She nodded, fear rushing through her body. How had she not seen this? How had she not known? Had she been too blind? Could she have prevented this from happening had she reacted earlier? Was she at fault for what happened to the Blacks' boy? They had tried to tell her about Anna Mae, hadn't they? They had all known, but she had refused to see it. Blinded by her love for the child and the unbearable fear of losing her, the closest she had ever come to having a child.

"As soon as she shows up, I'll make sure she is brought to you," she said, her eyes avoiding his, guilt gnawing in the pit of her stomach. "As soon as I find her."

The sheriff placed a hand on her shoulder. "I'm sorry, Carol, that it had to come to this. I know you care for the girl."

She nodded, staring at her shoes in the high grass. "Me too. I am more sorry than anyone, Sheriff."

50

I DIDN'T LIKE HAVING TO LEAVE, NOT WITHOUT GETTING MY story or even finding the truth. It wasn't very much like me, and as said my goodbyes to Adeline and her daughter, Regina, who were both behind the counter the next day when I came down, I felt a little like I was giving up. It wasn't a pleasant feeling. It was like the bad guy had won.

I paid for the room and told Adeline and Regina to take good care of one another, then left the motel, car keys jingling in my hand. As I reached the parking lot, I couldn't help but think about my run-in with Mr. Cunningham not too long ago in that same spot. A shiver ran down my spine when remembering the look in his eyes. He had told me to leave, and now I was giving him exactly what he wanted.

I walked to my car, pulling the suitcase behind me. I opened the trunk of the car with one click of the remote. I lifted the suitcase to put it in when I saw something that immediately made me drop the bag onto the pavement and start to scream.

I gasped for air, then pulled backward, still screaming.

Adeline and Regina came running out to the parking lot where they found me.

"What happened? What's going on?" Regina asked when she saw my face. I pointed, gasping between breaths, and stepped backward.

When they spotted the body in the trunk, they recoiled as well, mouths clasped, shrieks emerging from between their lips.

Regina walked to the car, then closed the trunk, slamming it shut. I stood like I was frozen, staring at the back of the car, still seeing the body even though the trunk was closed.

"I'm calling the sheriff," Adeline said, her voice shivering. She ran inside, and Regina came up to me.

"Come over here and sit down," she said and guided me to a bench leaned up against the wall. My legs were shaking so badly I could hardly walk and had to lean on her the entire way. My phone was still on the asphalt where I had dropped it out of my hand when opening the trunk. Regina picked it up and handed it to me as I heard sirens approaching in the distance.

In the minutes that followed, everything was a blur. My heart beat so loudly in my ears that I could hardly hear it when people spoke to me. All I could see were those eyes staring back at me from inside the trunk; all I could hear was my own blood rushing through my veins, my heart beating so fast I feared it would never calm down again.

Someone was in front of me, wearing khaki colored pants. He bent down and looked at me.

"Ms. Franck?"

I managed to nod when I recognized the man as Sheriff Travers.

"Is that your vehicle?" he asked. "Ma'am? Is that your car right there?"

I lifted my gaze and looked toward the car. The trunk was open again, and several uniformed people were looking inside it. Some of them were trying to get the body out, and soon they succeeded. They placed him on a tarp on the ground. An ambulance had arrived too, and a man I assumed had to be the coroner attended to the body.

"I need you to work with me here, Ms. Franck," Sheriff Travers said firmly. "Is this your vehicle?"

I nodded again. "Y-yes."

"And will you be so kind as to explain to me what exactly the body of this man is doing inside of your vehicle?"

I looked up and locked eyes with the sheriff. What was this? Did he think I had placed the body there?

"I…I…I don't know. How am I supposed to know that? I just came out here and…was about to leave and then…I opened the trunk to put my suitcase in and there he was."

"Did you know this man?" the sheriff asked.

"No. I have never seen him before in my life."

Sheriff Travers nodded and wrote notes on his pad.

"Y-you don't think that I…That I…?"

"Right now, I don't think anything, Ms. Franck, but in all fairness, he was found inside your trunk. I say you better stay in town for a few more days. I'll be calling you in for questioning as soon as the crime scene techs are done here."

51

"A̲ʟʟᴀɴ C̲ᴜɴɴɪɴɢʜᴀᴍ, ᴀʟsᴏ ᴋɴᴏᴡɴ ᴀʀᴏᴜɴᴅ ʜᴇʀᴇ ᴀs ᴛʜᴇ former Cucumber King, aged ninety-two."

Sheriff Travers pushed a photo toward me, sliding it across the table. It was later in the day, and I was still quite shaken, but at least I had calmed down a little now, enough to think.

I glanced briefly at the photo of the dead man in front of me. The sight made me sick.

"His throat was slit open using a fish-gutting knife. We found the bloody knife inside his kitchen when searching his house," the sheriff continued. His eyes were studying me while he spoke. They were constantly scrutinizing me, making me feel uncomfortable.

"I…I have never seen him before," I said.

"How do you explain him suddenly showing up in your trunk, might one ask?"

I shrugged. How could I answer that? "I have no idea. Someone must have placed him there. That's the only explanation that I can come up with."

"And why would someone do that?"

"Uh, to make it look like I killed him?" I said.

"Or maybe you did kill him," the sheriff said. "Maybe it's as simple as that. Who else would have access to your car keys?"

"I...I don't know."

"Well, who does know, Ms. Franck?"

"Listen, I don't know where this body came from. I was in my motel room all day yesterday. I only left to go eat at the Framer's Market, and the day before that, I went to visit Margot Addington in the hospital."

The sheriff bit his lip. "Been hanging out an awful lot with her lately, haven't you?"

"I interviewed her, yes. I went to visit her at the hospital because I thought she might need someone to talk to after losing her family in that fire. But she didn't want to talk to me, so I left."

"That fire was arson," he said. "Did she tell you that? Did she tell you how she removed the batteries of the fire alarms before setting the house on fire?"

My eyes grew wide. "Excuse me?"

"Well, that's my theory at least. They found two fire alarms at the site. They were melted, but they could still see that there were no batteries in them. That's why they didn't go off. I think she killed her entire family, but I can't prove it. At least not yet."

I sank back in my chair. Had Margot tried to commit suicide and taken the family with her? Was she capable of killing her own husband and daughter? Could the sheriff be right about her? Could they all be right? Was she a killer?

"Did you kill him?" the sheriff said. "Did you kill Allan Cunningham and place him in your trunk?"

"No! I would never do that. I'm telling you; someone framed me for this," I said. "Can't you see it?"

"They all say that," the sheriff said. "You had a little dispute with his son-in-law earlier in the week, didn't ya? I say you got upset with the young Mr. Cunningham and decided to teach him a little lesson. Taking out the old man was just easier."

I shook my head. I couldn't believe it.

"This is ridiculous."

The sheriff lifted his eyebrows. He gathered the photos, then rose to his feet. "We'll have to see about that. I'm letting you go for now, but don't leave town."

52

"THERE SHE IS. I CAN'T BELIEVE THE SHERIFF JUST LET HER go like that."

The words fell as I walked inside the Farmer's Market that same night. The smell of fried chicken and cornbread hit my nostrils, and I was starving, but as I saw all the eyes staring at me and noticed how the chatter died down as I entered, I lost my appetite.

I sat at a booth, and the waitress came up to me. She gave me one of those looks, telling me she was only talking to me out of sheer duty. She would rather be caught dead than be seen talking to me otherwise.

"I'll just have some sweet tea, please, and the buffet," I said without looking at her.

"As you wish," she said, then turned around and disappeared. I wondered if my glass would come back with spit in it, but then figured even the people of Webster weren't that cruel. The waitress brought me the tea, and I sipped it, while all eyes still lingered on me.

I grabbed my plate, then walked to the buffet. Low

voices whispered as I walked past their tables, and I hurried. I stopped by the fried chicken and grabbed a piece when an old woman came up to me. She poked me with her cane, and I turned to look.

"What…?"

Her squinting eyes stared up at me. "Allan Cunningham was a very loved man around here. Did a lot of good for the entire community. A church-man too."

"I'm sure he was," I said. "I'm sure he was a wonderful man."

"He and his family have been around here for a very long time."

"Again, I'm sure…"

The cane was lifted again. "This is a nice town. We don't like trouble around here."

"I'm sure you don't. Last time I looked, I hadn't caused any. And as far as I know, I am still innocent till proven guilty. I think that still counts even around here. Now, if you'll excuse me, I would like to get something to eat. It's been a pretty terrible day."

"Norma, behave."

The woman turned around as Regina and Adeline came up to me. Adeline smiled and grabbed plates for herself and her daughter.

"Go ahead," she said to me. "Get some food. They won't bother you again, or they'll have to answer to me."

"Thanks," I said, feeling suddenly very homesick. I hated it here. I loathed the way they all looked at me and talked about me, believing I had killed someone. How was I ever going to get out of this place? It was like it had sucked me in and wouldn't let me go.

I had called Sune right after I was let out of the sheriff's office and let him know what was going on, crying between words. He had told me he'd stay with the kids and not to worry. He had also told me he would try and get a good lawyer for me and that Kim could help him. She knew someone.

Of course, it all came down to her. Of course, I had to put my life in the hands of my ex-boyfriend's new girl-friend. If this was a joke, I wasn't finding it very funny.

I sat with Regina and Adeline for the rest of the dinner, while they desperately tried to make small talk to help me feel better. I sensed Regina wasn't as convinced about my innocence as her mother was, but I couldn't really hold it against her. I knew how it looked.

After dinner, I walked back to the motel along with them and said goodnight in the lobby before walking back to my room. From my bed, I called Julie and talked to William as well, crying while I spoke to them, but holding it back enough not to let them know. When I was done, I hung up and closed my eyes for a few seconds, as some-thing was slid under my door. I walked to it and found a note. When I opened it, I saw just one word written on it:

MURDERER

I crumpled the note up and threw it out, then—feeling angry and determined—I sat down at my computer. I couldn't just let this happen to me and not do anything about it. I couldn't just sit here and wait while the world fell apart around me. I had to act.

So, I opened my laptop and opened all the documents I had on the conviction of Anna Mae Burke back in seventy-nine. Then I searched for new articles written about her and how she was convicted of double murder at the age of only ten years old.

I was convinced there had to be some connection between what happened back then and now. There simply had to be. I thought that if only I dug deeper, then maybe I would also find a connection to the murder of Allan Cunningham. There had to be something connecting them, and I was determined to find it, even if it meant staying up all night.

53

WEBSTER, FLORIDA 1979

They held a town meeting at City Hall. Carol felt terrible sitting in those hard chairs listening to them talk about Anna Mae and what to do about her. But it was necessary that they stuck together now, the sheriff urged, and not let panic get the better of them.

"Two children are dead, Sheriff," Sandra, who worked at the Farmer's Market said, standing to her feet. "How many more need to be killed before you arrest her? How long do I have to fear for my own children's safety?"

"It is still an ongoing investigation," he said. "I'm afraid we don't have much evidence yet, at least not enough to get her convicted."

Anna Mae had gone back to stay at her mother's house. After she disappeared from the lot where they found Benjamin Black, Joanna had called Carol and asked her what her daughter was suddenly doing back there. Carol had told her the entire story and said she couldn't have her at her house anymore. She simply didn't dare to. She had been locking the doors at night and slept with one eye open in case the girl tried to get back in. Carol wasn't proud of herself, but she had to admit she feared Anna Mae and what she was capable of. Part of her wished the girl had run away and that she would never come back. It would make it so much easier on all of them if she did.

"How can you not have enough evidence?" the local auto mechanic, Bill Newman asked. "It sounds pretty simple to me. She knew where the body was. Only the murderer could have known where the body was. Carol, tell them."

All eyes were on Carol now, and she rose slowly to her feet, then cleared her throat.

"I think Bill is right," she said. "She made that drawing and showed me where it was, and to be…"

"See?" Bill said. "How is that not enough? What more can you possibly need?"

The crowd agreed, murmuring to one another.

Sheriff Waters calmed them down. "That's not how it works, folks," he said. "And you know it. We've had Anna Mae in for questioning several times, but she doesn't say anything. We can't place her at the scene of the crime; no one saw the two of them together on the day he disappeared. Now, we all feel pretty confident that Anna Mae did kill both Timmy and Benjamin, but I still need time to gather evidence against her. The last thing we want is for an innocent little girl to go to prison."

"Innocent?" The Cucumber King, Allan Cunningham said, rising to his feet. "How can you call her innocent when we all know what she has done? She even signed the darn body with her initial."

"Anyone could have done that," the sheriff said. "I'm not saying she's innocent, just that the evidence needs to be there."

"If it's not there, then that must mean you're not doing

your job properly, Sheriff," the Cucumber King continued. "Even her own aunt knows she did it. I say we lock her up once and for all, right now. We'll go to Joanna's house and bring her in."

The crowd murmured again, all agreeing. Sheriff Waters rubbed his forehead.

"I refuse to put a young girl behind bars and ruin her life unless I am five-hundred percent sure she did it," he said. "I'm telling you, no jury will convict her with what we have so far. Now, if you'll excuse me, I have to get back to work."

Sheriff Waters stepped down from the podium and began to walk away. The crowd rose to their feet in anger and yelled at him as he rushed out the back door. Carol watched their clenched fists and angry faces, sinking deeper and deeper into her chair.

In the corner, she spotted Deputy Travers and the Cucumber King deeply engrossed in a conversation, their serious eyes lingering on her as they spoke.

54

"It's been a while since anyone asked me about that old case. Do you mind if I ask what your interest is in it?"

Old Sheriff Waters' grey eyes lingered on me. We were sitting in his living room at his house that was only a few feet down the street from the motel, close enough for me to walk there.

I had called him the same morning and asked if he had time to talk to me, for research reasons, for a story I was doing about Webster and how it had been affected by the death of Timmy Peterson and Benjamin Black back in the seventies.

"I guess I just wanted to know more once I heard about it. I came here to interview Margot Addington for *Metropolitan Magazine*, and then they found the body of Alexander Cunningham in the old abandoned house. That's when I heard about what happened back then, and it caught my attention. I wanted to write about it. Especially now that they found out that Margot Addington is actually Anna Mae Burke, and all the old wounds have been ripped open once again."

Sheriff Waters leaned back in his creaking leather recliner with a sigh. "Terrible story that one was. Worst case in my entire career."

"I'm sure it was," I said. "Now, just to get my facts straight. Anna Mae Burke was convicted of murdering both boys," I said. "In seventy-nine. She was only ten years old at that time, and yet she was put in prison with adults, where she spent the next twenty years of her life among some of the worst criminals in our state. From what I've read about the case, you were certain it was her, but lacked evidence, am I right?"

The sheriff nodded. "Yes. That was the hard part. We had the drawings she had made, but that wasn't quite enough. I mean, the entire town was talking about these killings and especially the kids. There's nothing unusual about a child being fascinated by it and making drawings of it. It's creepy, but not that unusual."

"Except Anna Mae drew exactly where one of the boys was before he was found, right?"

"Yes. That's when everyone realized it had to be her and demanded that we prosecute her."

"But the drawing and the fact that she had led her own aunt to where the boy was still wasn't enough to hold up in court," I said.

"No, it wasn't. And the girl wouldn't tell us anything. She shut up like a clam every time we brought her in. She would just stare at us while her fingers rubbed against one another; sometimes, she would even grin eerily when we showed her pictures of the dead boys. It was spooky. She was a very creepy child. But it was no wonder with that mother of hers."

"She was abusive?" I asked, remembering reading about her mother being a prostitute.

"It was more than that. She tried to kill Anna Mae on

numerous occasions. She forced her to eat pills, sending Anna Mae to the hospital again and again. And then she had all those men coming to the house constantly, screwing her for money. It's no wonder the child was messed up. Her aunt took her in for a few months, but it was too late, the damage had been done. I felt for the girl; I really did, and I guess part of me wanted her to be innocent, but she murdered those boys, and there wasn't anything I could do to help her. I had to look at the facts and see behind that pretty face and those innocent blue eyes. Up until then, I would never have thought a child could kill another child, but I guess evil comes in all shapes and colors."

"What I haven't been able to figure out is exactly how you did that. I think my readers might like to know. You said you had no hard evidence, so how did you manage to get her convicted anyway?"

The old man sank back in his chair. He gave me a look that made me think there were parts of him that still doubted the girl's guilt. It was only there for a few seconds before it left.

"Fibers," he said. "They found fibers on the bodies of both boys. Both yellowish-green nylon fibers that matched the carpets at her Aunt Carol's house along with violet acetate fibers that matched the bedspreads at Carol's house. Her house was where Anna Mae lived at the time that she killed Benjamin Black, and she went there often and spent the night there when Timothy Peterson was killed. It is very unlikely that anyone else would have that exact combination of fibers in their homes, the prosecutor argued, and that's how we finally nailed her."

He said the last words with an air of disgust like he didn't find pleasure in having done so. I couldn't blame him. It couldn't have been pleasant to have to "nail" a young girl like that. You'd have to be completely convinced that she was guilty.

"I think I still have the old box in the back," he suddenly said and rose to his feet. "Give me a second, will you?"

I nodded and followed him into a small office that looked like it hadn't been used in a very long time. Old newspapers were piled up on the floors; books were spread out on the desk, which also held an old dusty stationary computer.

"Here it is," Sheriff Waters said and pulled out a box. He blew dust off it and smiled. "This is all the paperwork from the case. The police report, the arrest report and arrest log, transcripts from our interrogations of Anna Mae, and all the notes we took. It's available to the public, so I'm entitled to show it to you. Maybe you can use it for something."

He held the box out, and I took it, quite surprised. It was limited what was available online from back then.

"Thank you."

He smiled, then nodded. "No problem."

Sheriff Waters walked me out and held the door for me. I stopped as I was about to cross the threshold.

"One last question."

He nodded. "Yes?"

"Would you say that you have no doubt in your mind that Anna Mae Burke killed those two boys?" I asked this, knowing it was going to be a difficult question for him.

He thought it over for quite some time, his upper lip vibrating slightly. Then he shook his head.

"I have no doubt," he said heavily. "I can't allow myself to. What good would that do me or anyone else for that matter?"

55

I walked back holding the box with a strange feeling seeping through my body. I couldn't escape what Sheriff Waters had said to me. It wasn't what he said; it was more the way he said it.

The man wasn't sure about Anna Mae's guilt. He couldn't say that to my face; of course, he couldn't, so that was why he hinted at it instead, and that was also why he had given me this box.

He hoped I could somehow get to the truth. I wondered if it was the death of Alexander Cunningham that had ripped up the doubt in him. Did he know his death was no accident? Or had it just brought back too many memories and made him doubt what they had concluded back then?

Either way, I was getting even more certain that I was approaching the truth, and whatever it was, it was ugly enough for people to lie about it and cover it up.

I smiled at Regina, who was sweeping outside the motel, then felt her eyes on me as I walked back to the room. I knew they were all on their toes around me, thinking I had killed the old Cucumber King, and I was expecting to be picked up by the sheriff's deputies any moment now to be brought in for more ridiculous questioning.

I had spoken to Kim's friend, the lawyer, earlier the same morning, and she told me she could help me out, but I had to stay put to show my willingness to cooperate. When they called me in for my next interrogation, I'd have to call her, so she could come with me. She lived about an hour away.

Back in my room, I found a pack of cookies I had bought earlier in the week at Circle K and opened it, thinking that would have to be my lunch. For breakfast, I had eaten a granola bar that I had lying around. I was trying to stay away from the Farmer's Market after last night's failure, and since I didn't have a car because it had been taken to forensics, there really weren't that many places to get something to eat. Regina and Adeline had told me I could go with them to the market for dinner, but I wasn't sure I was up to it once again. I couldn't stand those staring eyes and all that whispering behind my back. It made me feel like the loneliest person on the planet.

I closed the door behind me and sat down on the bed with the box. Then I opened it and pulled out one old yellow folder after another. They had lost a lot of color and felt like they could turn to dust any second now, but the papers inside of them were in good shape. Good enough for me to be able to read. I went through the arrest records and the log, where Anna Mae's picture was attached on the top, her blue eyes staring back at me from behind the bangs. It was hard to believe it was the same person as Margot Addington, but the eyes gave her away.

I put the records aside, then opened another folder, the one with the transcripts from her interviews. There were many pages, and I leaned back, then began to read through them. For the most part, it was Sheriff Waters and Deputy Travers who did the talking, asking one question after another, like where she had been on the day when Timothy Peterson disappeared. To that, Anna Mae simply answered, "Around." And it went on like that for page after page. They would ask her a question, and she would answer with just a nod or shaking her head or just one word. Sometimes, she simply didn't say or do anything at all. She just stared at her shoes, it said in the notes.

It must have driven them nuts.

Finally, after hours of reading through the material, I stumbled on something that made me stop and reread it over and over again. I lifted my gaze and stared at her picture on the top of the file, while a piece of the puzzle suddenly fell into place, whispering:

"Oh, my God."

56

Sheriff Leon Travers belched. Christina, his wife of twenty-five years, looked up from her plate.

"Sorry," he said.

She gave him one of her warming smiles, and he was lost for a second in her eyes. The sadness in them felt like knives to his heart. In them was the longing for something he hadn't been able to give her, and it tormented him every day of his life.

"I was done anyway," Christina said as she grabbed both his and her own plate and left for the kitchen. His eyes lingered on the doorway long after she had left him.

They had tried for years, but that child that they wanted so desperately simply hadn't come and even though it was long ago that they had given up on ever conceiving, it was still this thing between them that they couldn't escape.

"Do you want dessert, Leon?" she yelled from the kitchen, even though they both knew it was a silly question.

When realizing they couldn't have any children, Christina had drowned her sorrow with excessive cleaning, and to this day, the house was still spotlessly clean, and every piece of clothing was neatly folded inside Leon's closet. Meanwhile, Leon had thrown himself at pie or anything else that was sweet enough to subdue the pain. And for the past fifteen years at least, his weight had simply gone only one way: up and up again. It wasn't something Leon was very proud of. He had stopped looking at himself in the mirror and sex wasn't even on the agenda anymore. Leon knew how Christina looked at him. He knew how she felt about his weight gain, even though she tried to hide her stares and only did it when she believed he wasn't looking. Still, he knew. He disgusted her and probably everyone else around them.

"I made an apple pie," she said, peeking her head out.

Leon smiled, his eyes swimming at the thought of a sizzling warm piece of home-baked apple pie. What could be better in this world?

"Sounds delicious," he said. "I could eat some of that."

She served him a piece with whipped cream, and he dug in, pressing back the thoughts that had been ripped up in his mind lately and wouldn't go away, no matter how much he tried to keep them out. It was all because of that stupid journalist. If only she hadn't come here and talked about Alexander's autopsy report, then he would have believed he'd be able to get away with his little lie. He knew it wasn't fair to Alexander's parents. They deserved to know the truth, but he had to do it. Only he would understand why, and that was what hurt so much. Fact was, if the truth was revealed, he would lose everything, and he couldn't risk that happening.

"I'm going to check on Deborah," Christina said as she grabbed her purse and car keys. "I'm taking her some food."

Deborah Murphy was Christina's good friend who

lived down the street from them. She had recently been sick from some type of throat cancer that Leon had never heard of, and since she was all alone, Christina felt obligated to take care of her. She took food to her every night to make sure she got something decent to eat. It was important for her to regain her strength, Christina said.

"But I'm leaving the apple pie on the counter," she said. "In case you want another piece."

Leon nodded while shoveling in the warm pie, then gazed after his wife as she left the house, smiling at the thought of how well she knew him.

As soon as she was gone, he trotted to the kitchen where the rest of the pie was resting on the counter. With the spoon tightly in his grip, he threw himself at it, gobbling the rest of it down, eating so much his stomach ended up hurting.

Belching again, holding a hand to his painful stomach, he went to the living room and threw himself on the couch, hoping a little downtime would end up clearing him of this pain, yet knowing deep inside that the pain would never go away. The stomachache would, but not the rest. The rest, he had to live with till the day he died.

He just didn't realize that moment might come a lot sooner than he had expected. It wasn't until he heard the footsteps, then opened his eyes, gasping, and looked into the ones of his killer, that he knew it.

"Please," he whispered.

But his words were in vain. He knew they would be, yet he tried. His killer didn't care, though. Instead, she leaned over, looked straight into his eyes, then lifted the knife, and before Leon could move his massive body, she brought it down to his chest, piercing it straight through his flesh and into his heart. As blood gushed out of him, she leaned over and whispered close to his ear:

"It ends here."

57

I borrowed Adeline's truck, telling her I needed to go buy some food, and drove through town, my heart pounding in my chest. I reached Sheriff Travers' house and parked in the driveway, then rushed to the door. I knocked, then knocked again when no one opened the door. As I did, the door slid open, and that was when I heard it. Gurgling sounds were coming from inside the living room, and it sounded like someone was choking.

"Sheriff Travers?" I asked and stepped cautiously in over the threshold, holding the transcripts in my hand. I had brought them to show the sheriff what I had found.

"Hello?"

I walked inside and found Sheriff Travers on the couch, blood gushing down onto the carpet below, a knife still stuck in his chest.

"Oh, my God, Sheriff?" I said and hurried to him. "Sheriff? Are you still there? What happened?"

He was still alive, but barely. He was sputtering and fighting to breathe. "Hang in there," I said, then grabbed my phone from my pocket. "I'm calling for help."

As I fumbled with the phone nervously, he lifted his bloody hand and grabbed my arm. Startled I turned to look, then realized he was trying to say something.

Trying to calm my poor beating heart, I leaned closer while our eyes locked, panic rushing through his. His mouth moved, and he tried to speak. Blood spilled from his lips when he whispered with a hoarse voice:

"Anna Mae…is…"

Mid-sentence, his hand let go of my shirt, and the sheriff's massive body sank down while life left his eyes. The sight made me start to cry.

"No! Sheriff Travers, no!"

I pressed his chest, trying to perform CPR, but there was nothing that helped. Tapping the screen frantically, I called 911.

"Hello? I need an ambulance; someone was murdered. Please, come quickly; he's not breathing anymore. There's no pulse."

After giving them the address, I knelt next to him, crying, waiting for the ambulance to arrive. While sitting on the floor, I realized how it would look if the police found me there. I was a suspect in a murder case, for the murder of another of the town's big men, and I had a vested interest in getting rid of the sheriff. Someone might think I had killed him.

A sudden panic set in. I gathered my things, then ran out the front door, desperately looking in the direction of the sirens, then got into Adeline's truck and drove off, tires screeching on the asphalt. I knew it was very risky what I was doing, but who would ever believe me? Even if I told them the truth, this story was a little too hard to believe. I had probably left DNA all over the scene and someone— possibly a neighbor—had most likely seen me run out of the house and take off. Plus, it was going to take them like five minutes to find out I was the one who had called for help. My voice was on tape, and the call came from my own phone. It wasn't going to take them long to come for me, but right now, I didn't care much about all that. I had to go find Anna Mae, and fast. With what I had found in the papers and what the sheriff had said before he died, I had a feeling I was right on track.

58

WEBSTER, FLORIDA 1979

When the first day of the trial came, everyone in town had a story to tell about Anna Mae. Events from all the way back early in her childhood were brought into the light on that hot summer day in July in the Sumter County Courthouse.

One after another, the people in Anna Mae's life took the stand and told what they knew about the girl. There were stories about how she had fought with other girls, both in and out of school, how she had once forced a friend to eat sand till she almost choked, and how she had drawn a picture of the dead body of Timothy in class, scaring the teacher.

The Petersons' story probably made the biggest impression on that day. Mrs. Peterson took the stand and told the jury how the girl had tormented them after losing their son, how she had come to their house, an eerie grin on her face and asked if they missed him, if they were crying at night. How she had asked to see the body of Timothy in the coffin.

"I just couldn't believe a child could do this to us," Mrs. Peterson said. "No one can be that cruel, especially not a child."

Carol was then asked to take the stand, and while trying hard to not look directly at Anna Mae, she told the jury how she had seen Anna Mae torture animals, how she had been acting strangely after the death of Timothy, and also how she had led her to the body of Benjamin Black after she had seen her drawing.

"As much as I hate to say this because I care for the child, I truly do, but something isn't right with her."

As she said the words, her eyes fell on Anna Mae, and Carol burst into tears. She had loved the girl, she really had, but it was out of her hands now. She couldn't lie in court, and to be honest, she wanted Anna Mae to be put away. The girl scared her more than ever.

After the first day of the trial, Carol went home to her house and locked the doors thoroughly, then sunk to her knees, crying. She felt so helpless. Earlier in the day, she had heard the chief medical examiner talk about how he believed both boys had been killed by someone putting pressure to their throats and blocking the airways, just by using their fingers.

"Only a child's fingers could leave no bruise," he added.

Carol couldn't stop thinking about those two poor boys, so young, so fragile, and so innocent. Timothy had been five, Benjamin only four years old. And then she kept picturing Anna Mae luring them to go with her, telling them she had candy or to come play. She could imagine her as she grabbed their throats, as soon as they were alone, and then she pictured her as she was hovering above them, looking down at them with her eerie little smile, and pressing her thumbs down on their throats till they stopped breathing. Just like she had done to that poor bird in Carol's backyard.

How could a child possess such cruelty?

A knock on her door made Carol wipe her eyes and get to her feet. She opened the door and outside stood two men she knew very well.

"Allan? Leon?"

The seriousness in their eyes made Carol's heart drop. "We're losing the trial," Allan Cunningham said. "We're going to lose."

"There isn't enough evidence, according to the prosecutor," Deputy Travers continued. "She'll walk if we don't do something about it."

"We have to do something," Allan Cunningham added. "Now."

The thought made Carol's heart start to pound. This couldn't be happening. Anna Mae couldn't walk free after this. She had to be put away; she simply had to. Carol couldn't bear the guilt she was carrying from the death of those two boys. What if Anna Mae was let out and there were more? No, they had to put her away. There was no other solution.

"But…but…what can we do about it? Is there anything I can do?"

They looked briefly at one another, then back at her.

"We might have an idea. Can we come in?"

59

It had started to rain, and when it rained in Florida, it poured. The wipers on Adeline's truck creaked as they slid across the windshield and cleared away the water, yet the road in front of me was still hard to see. I had to squint and lean forward as I drove out of town toward the Addington estate.

I accelerated as soon as I was past the city limit sign, then sped through the landscape, splashing through big puddles of water, hoping and praying that I wasn't going to skid off the road.

Halfway there, my phone rang. The display lit up with Sune's name on it, and I had to pick it up in case it was something with the kids.

"What's wrong?" I said, holding the phone between my shoulder and ear while concentrating on steering the truck through the darkness. "What happened?"

"Does something have to be wrong for me to call you?" he asked. "Can't I just call you anymore?"

"No, no, of course, you can," I said. "I'm sorry. I'm a little stressed out right now; that's all. How are the kids?"

"The kids are fine. They miss you, though. Especially Tobias," Sune said.

My heart ached. It had to be hard on the boy. Even though he wasn't my son, Sune already had him when I met him, and I loved the kid like he was my own. When Sune and I split up, he had come to me and told me he was scared he'd never see me again. I told him I was going to be there for him just as much as for Julie and William, but I could tell he didn't fully believe me.

"Tell him I miss him too," I said and made a turn, the truck skidding sideways. I got it back on track with a shriek, missing a tall skinny palm tree by a few inches.

"Rebekka? Are you okay? What's going on? Are you driving?"

"Yes, I am…"

"Where are you going, Rebekka? Why do I have a feeling you're getting yourself into trouble again?" he asked.

"I'm just…I need to do this, Sune. I have to," I said, hoping that he would accept this as an explanation. I couldn't go into detail right now; I didn't have time. I didn't really want to either. He would only get angry with me.

"Are you on the run from the police or something? Rebekka, you're scaring me. What the heck is going on there?"

"Listen, Sune, I'll have to explain later," I said and spotted the gate leading to the Addington estate, or what was left of it since the fire truck blasted through it the other day. I continued up the road leading to the house, driving between the tall trees that seemed to have grown more vicious-looking since I was there last. The horses were in the field, and the sound of me approaching in the truck startled them.

"Don't hang up on me, Rebekka. I need you to…"

I stopped the truck in the driveway, close to the house, or what was left of it, then killed the engine.

"I have to go now, Sune. I'll call you later."

"Reb…"

I hung up, then shut off my phone. Sune would have to wait till later. I couldn't deal with him right now. Besides, it wasn't a good idea to have my phone turned on once the police started to look for me.

The rain had slowed down a little but still fell hard from the dark sky above. I got out of the truck, and by the time I reached the remains of the burnt down house, I was already soaked. Water was dripping from my hair into my face, and my shirt felt clammy on my chest and arms. It didn't matter, though. The rain was warm, and to be honest, I didn't care much right now. All I cared about was finding Margot Addington in time.

I rushed past the ruins of the burnt down house and ran into the stables where I could keep dry. I shook my head to get the water out of my hair.

"Margot?" I called.

All the stalls were empty, and the horses were still running around outside in the field. It didn't look like anyone had cleaned the stalls out for days, but the horses had been fed. There was food in the troughs.

Margot had to have been back there since the fire.

I walked through the stables and peeked outside on the other side of them, where I spotted a small wooden house in the back that hadn't been destroyed in the fire. It was raining hard again now, so I ran there, my poor shoes and jeans getting soaked in the puddles I stepped in on the way.

As I reached the house, I knocked.

"Margot? Are you in there? Margot?"

When no answer came, I grabbed the handle and opened the door.

"Margot?" I said and stepped inside.

There was a bed pressed up against the end wall and a small restroom in the back. A table in the middle had the local newspaper spread out on top of it. I walked closer and spotted an article about the falling cucumber prices. From the photo, taken in the middle of their cucumber field, Mr. and Mrs. Cunningham stared back at me.

60

Mrs. Cunningham stood in the doorway to her son's room. Everything was still in the same place as it had been before he disappeared. The bed was unmade, and the covers with the airplanes on them were hanging over the edge, half of it lying on the carpet. His favorite teddy bear was the only one sleeping in the bed now, while his new truck was standing on the shelf, gathering dust. A couple of books were spread out on the floor, and Mrs. Cunningham thought to herself that she really ought to get them cleaned up, but she couldn't get herself to. She hadn't dared to go in there yet, and she still didn't. She wasn't ready for it; she wasn't ready to accept that her little boy was gone.

A fond memory of him drawing on the walls with his crayons and her yelling at him for doing so swept her mind, and she chuckled sadly. There would be no new memories to make. There would be no annoying teenager in the house, yelling at them and slamming doors for no apparent reason. Nor would there be any graduation pictures or calls in the middle of the night telling them to come get him because he had too much to drink at some party. There would be no wedding or foolish daughter-in-law that she could disapprove of. There would be no grandchildren that she could spoil, and there would be no one to take over the family business.

Now, her father was gone too, the old bastard. Less than a week after they had found Alexander's body in that abandoned house, he had been killed, murdered. That one was no accident; she knew that much. He had been found in the trunk of that strange woman's car, the reporter who was living out at the motel, the sheriff had told her. She was dangerous, he had also said, and he hoped to be able to put her away for a very long time.

Mrs. Cunningham was still shivering at the thought of her coming to the farm and talking all that nonsense about Alexander being murdered and not having an accident. She had been so convincing that Mrs. Cunningham had found herself doubting what she had been told, and she had asked her husband about it when they were about to go to bed that same night.

"Could the sheriff be wrong?" she had asked. "Could he have lied to us?"

That was when her husband got angry. He had taken up the book on his nightstand, the one about the life of Johnny Carson, then thrown it across the room. Mrs. Cunningham had thought it was very odd behavior on her husband's part. Very unlike him. Ever since Sheriff Travers had been at their door and had given them the terrible news about Alexander, Mr. Cunningham had remained very quiet. He had barely uttered a word ever since then, but now he did. Now he yelled at her and threw his book across the room.

"Why would you say something like that, huh? Why?" he almost screamed. "Does it make a difference if he was murdered? He is gone. Gone. There is nothing that will ever bring him back. Nothing."

After that, she hadn't brought it up again. She had decided that the journalist had been wrong. After all, it made more sense to trust their local sheriff than some journalist passing through town. And when it all came down to it, she knew it couldn't be the same killer as it had been back then, back when they were children. It couldn't be the same person that had killed Timothy Peterson and Benjamin Black. That much she was certain of.

But then they had started talking about Anna Mae being back and living outside of town under another name, and that had shaken her even deeper. If Anna Mae was back, there was no telling what she might do. Mr. Cunningham knew nothing about this because he wasn't here back then. He moved to town when he married Mrs. Cunningham, and when her dad retired, that was when he became the new Cucumber King of Webster, a title that came with the job. He took her name since it came with such deep traditions, and the old Cucumber King wanted the name to live on and stay with the farm.

Now that Alexander wasn't anymore, there would be no more cucumber kings in town. Mrs. Cunningham had Alexander late in life, and he was their miracle baby after plenty of fertility treatments and almost giving up. Now, she was too old to have any more children, so it was all going to end with them.

Mrs. Cunningham closed the door to her son's room and wiped away a tear from the corner of her eye. Mr. Cunningham was out tonight, and she realized he had been out a lot lately, and that she didn't know anything about what he was doing. She also realized that she didn't really care.

As she heard a car in the driveway, she thought it was

him, so she walked down to the bathroom downstairs and washed her face, so he wouldn't see that she had been crying. As the car door slammed shut outside, she sat down in a chair in the living room and grabbed her book, then pretended to be reading as the steps approached the front door. When the door opened, she prepared a smile to show him as he entered, trying to make him feel welcome, but as the door swung open and she saw who stood in the doorway, her smile froze in place, and her hands began to shake.

"You?"

"Yes, me. Have you missed me?"

61

I COULDN'T BELIEVE I HADN'T SEEN IT COMING. I SHOULD have; I kept scolding myself. I should have realized that Margot was up to something. As I rushed down the trail of the Addington estate toward the big road, I just hoped I wasn't going to be too late.

It all made sense now; well, not all of it, but a lot of it, I thought to myself as I took the turn onto 471 toward Webster. I was just annoyed with myself that I hadn't seen the connection before now.

It was still pouring like crazy, and I could hardly see the road ahead of me. The headlights of a car driving in the other direction blinded me as it passed me. I tried to drive faster but didn't feel safe, so I slowed down once again. In my rearview mirror, I spotted the car that had just passed me as it stopped, turned around, and came back my way.

"What the…?"

The car came up closer behind me and turned on its blinkers and a siren.

"Oh, no," I mumbled. "Just my luck."

My hands grew sweaty holding onto the wheel so

intensely. The cruiser behind me came closer and closer, siren blaring, while I tried to figure out what to do. It could just be a patrol seeing me speeding and wanting me to stop. It could be nothing but a speeding ticket. That was definitely a possibility, but what would happen if I did stop? They would run my license and plate, of course, they would, and then they'd know that there was a search out for the truck I was driving and me in connection with the murder of their sheriff.

Oh, my God. I'm gonna be on the news. They're all gonna think I murdered their beloved sheriff. They're gonna want to see me hang.

I stared at the road ahead of me, feeling my heart rate go up rapidly. The police cruiser was getting close now, too close for my comfort. I stared at it in the rearview mirror while biting my cheek, contemplating what to do.

You can't let them catch you, Rebekka. Then there'll be no one to stop Margot Addington. They'll never believe you. You have to deal with her first, then explain later.

"Oh, dear Lord," I mumbled. "Forgive me for what I am about to do."

I took one last glance in the rearview mirror, then made my decision. There was no time to hesitate now. I had to act, and so I did. I took in a deep breath, then pressed down on the accelerator, putting all my weight onto it. The truck jolted forward, and soon I was running at full speed, my heart pounding like a wild beast in my chest.

At full speed ahead, I rushed down the road, my eyes fully focused on the road ahead, but finding it hard to follow it properly at this speed. The truck skidded to the side in a turn, but I managed to get it back on the asphalt. Meanwhile, I looked desperately for an escape route, somehow to lose the cruiser behind me, who had also accelerated and was now following me with blasting sirens.

I was surrounded by the swamps on both sides as the road went straight through them. I didn't dare to leave the asphalt, even though I was driving a four-wheel-drive truck. I had no idea how to drive in terrain like that and would only get stuck somewhere.

A hill met me up ahead, and I rushed up it, then as we reached the top, the cruiser came up on my side. Heart in my throat, I made a rash decision, probably too rash, most people might say. I grabbed the wheel and turned it, causing the truck to run off the road and bumble into the swampy grass next to the road.

As I bounced downward, nothing but darkness ahead of me, I looked in the rearview mirror and saw that the cruiser had followed me. It wasn't giving up.

62

"Anna Mae…I…please…"

"It's Margot now," she said, holding the gun clutched between her fingers so tight they hurt. "Margot Addington is my name."

"Okay, Margot, I… Listen to me…"

Margot shook her head. She glanced at the picture of Mrs. Cunningham and her husband together on the dresser next to her and thought about Theodore for a brief second. They had been happy like that; they had been in love like those two were in that picture, maybe even more. And they'd had a beautiful daughter together, a daughter who could have grown up to become whatever she wanted, who could have gone to the best college because they could afford it. Against all odds, Margot had managed to create a good life for herself, one where her past didn't matter, where no one knew of it. Theodore had pulled her out of the poverty she had been born into, and their marriage had meant that she would be able to give her daughter the childhood she never had, that she had only been able to dream of.

But now it was all gone. Theodore was gone, Minna was gone, and so was her future. She would never write another book; she simply couldn't. There was nothing left for her on this Earth.

"Why did you come back here?" Mrs. Cunningham asked, shaking her head. "If only you had stayed away, no one would have found out. You could have kept living your life. You'd still have your family and your career. Why on Earth did you move here?"

Margot swallowed hard. The knuckles on the hand holding the gun were turning white. The safe from their bedroom was one of the things that had survived the fire, and in it, she had found the gun. It was funny because she had always been on Theodore's case, telling him she didn't want a weapon in her house, and that she was scared that her daughter might one day find it and accidentally shoot herself or a friend, like in all those stories you read online or heard about in the news. But Theodore had told her it was locked away safely, and he had been right. Ironically, it was the only thing that survived when even he didn't. Even the combination had worked when Margot plotted it in. There was also some cash in there that had made it, a couple of thousand dollars. She had used some of it to buy some new clothes and some food to eat since it had turned out that Theodore's credit card was cut off after he died. But there really wasn't much more she needed right now.

Except settling the score.

"I had no choice," Margot said. "Theodore got the offer to fill this position at Leesburg. It was a great opportunity for him. Until then, we were doing just fine. Living in New York was the dream. I wrote my books, Theodore had a great position at Morgan Stanley Children's Hospital, and Minna thrived in school. And then BAM came this offer, and he just accepted it without even asking me. He said he couldn't say no. It was too much money. Naturally, I was terrified since I didn't want to go back anywhere near Florida, but this was a huge break for him, and he said it would only be for a few years, then we could move back again. I accepted it because I had no choice. I could hardly tell him why I didn't want to go since then I'd have to tell him the truth, and he would have known I had been lying to him about my past. We found a place that was closer to Bushnell, and I truly believed I could stay under the radar. But then that foolish journalist called, and my stupid publishing house told me I had to do that interview. That it would be *oh-so-good* for my career. After that, everything went south."

Mrs. Cunningham stared at the gun, then up at Margot's face. Margot wondered if she could see how terribly her hands were shaking.

"I see," she said and leaned forward in her recliner. "And now you've come for me; I take it? First, you take out my father, and now me?"

63

THE TRUCK WAS MAKING STRANGE SOUNDS AS I RUSHED through the landscape, steering between trees and bushes, bumping along. Behind me, the cruiser was following a little too closely for my taste. I drove through an area of grass, at least that's what I thought it was, but I soon found out it was mostly wetland, and almost got stuck. Luckily the truck managed to pull itself out, mud spraying up behind me. It was terrifying to be rushing through the darkness, not knowing anything about where I was going, the cruiser blaring behind me. The grill of my truck hit some bushes that got stuck, and the engine roared to press through as I kept jamming on the accelerator. Mud skidded up behind me, hitting the cruiser.

"Come on," I yelled as the truck wasn't moving forward anymore. "Come on!"

The truck suddenly jolted forward again as it plowed through the thick vegetation. I screamed when it happened, startled at the sudden movement, and the truck bounced ahead, rushing through more wetlands, me losing complete control of it.

I looked in the rearview mirror and saw that the cruiser had stopped behind me, unable to force its way through the bushes that my truck had. Laughing victoriously, I grasped the steering wheel, clutching it hard, trying to regain control. A row of trees appeared suddenly in the headlights, and I screamed again, then turned the wheel, fast. The side view mirror hit the tree and was knocked off, and the side of the truck scraped across it, making an awful noise while I screamed my heart out.

Please, don't let me die here, God. Please!

The truck continued through the wetlands, bumping and splashing along, and I hit something that made the truck bounce off and shoot through the air, then land, splashing into deep water before it came to a complete and sudden stop.

I was thrown forward in the landing, then gasped for breath while I looked around me. I was surrounded by water, and it was coming inside the truck, making my feet wet.

"This is not good," I mumbled to myself. "This is definitely bad."

The engine had gone out, and I tried to restart it, but nothing happened. It didn't even cough.

"Come on; come on. Don't fail me now," I pleaded. Part of me was now regretting having left the police cruiser back there. I most certainly would be better off being hauled off to a cell somewhere than sitting here.

I slammed my hand into the wheel, then grabbed the key in the ignition and turned it again. The truck coughed a couple of times before it suddenly roared to life.

"That's my girl," I said, relieved. I pressed cautiously on the accelerator, making sure it didn't dig itself deeper into the mud instead of moving forward. The truck pushed itself slowly through the high water, and soon it came to more solid ground, and I could press a little more on the accelerator, while the water disappeared from inside the car and soon from around it as well.

I looked around me into the wilderness, then wondered where I was and how the heck I was supposed to find my way back. If I took a wrong turn, I might end up getting myself deeper into the swamps, and then I wouldn't be able to find my way back till daylight came.

If the gators didn't find me first.

64

I turned on my phone. I really didn't want to, but I had to in order to use the GPS. I could see nothing but darkness around me and knew that I could too easily get lost out here. Right now, I needed to be found or at least find out where I was.

The phone lit up in the darkness and soon turned on. Then it started buzzing in my hands as it alerted me that I had around a hundred text messages from Sune and many missed calls from him as well. I ignored them all, then opened the GPS to have it show me my location and hopefully show me if there was a road nearby.

The phone thought about it forever. Then a small sign told me there was poor connection and to please try again later. Annoyed, I cursed the phone, then tapped it harshly to try again, but it didn't work. It couldn't locate me. I was too deep into the swamps.

I threw it on the seat next to me, cursing myself for my little *Thelma and Louise* stunt, trying to outrun the police. I should have known better. I should have known that no good would ever come from running from the police. Now,

I was stuck out here in the darkness, and I had no idea what direction to go. I stared into the darkness with a deep sigh, then decided it was no use just to sit there and wait. I had to act. So, I turned the car in the direction I believed had to be toward the main road, then cautiously rolled forward. Outside, I could hear all the nightlife, birds tooting and animals crying in the night. I didn't know much about the swamps, but I did know that there were some pretty nasty creatures living out there, and I had to be careful not to run into any of them.

I had only driven a few yards when something was caught in my headlights. A big fat brownish pig-like creature stood on the trail in front of me, staring at me.

A wild hog.

It was as big as a small cow and looked to be about three hundred pounds, so I couldn't just run it down, I figured. Not without risking damaging the truck too. At least I didn't think I could, and I wasn't going to take any chances. It was sort of blocking my way, so I snuck the truck closer, hoping it would get out of my way when it saw me coming, but it didn't. It just stood there and stared at the headlights. I pressed down on the horn and honked at it, causing a couple of herons to lift off from nearby and fly away, making all kinds of strange noises. The hog still stood there like nothing had happened. I honked again, and some other animals rustled nearby, clever enough to run away. Finally, the big pig decided it was time to move on and walked away. I stared at it as it disappeared, then I laid my eyes on something else right next to me, close to the trail, lying in the grass.

A big fat gator.

Reminding myself of my last meeting with one and how it had left me with a deep scar in my thigh, I pressed down the gas pedal, then roared past it. Ever since I had almost lost my life to one, I had been terrified of gators, and I kept feeling its teeth as they sank into my skin.

I hit some thick bushes, then pressed the truck through it, heart pounding in my throat, and ended up in another grassy area. My hands were sweating heavily as I suddenly spotted headlights like small dots dancing in the far away darkness.

"Human life!" I exclaimed, then floored the pedal and took off toward it. I reached the road a few minutes later and drove up on the asphalt, feeling victorious. My GPS was working now, and I realized I wasn't very far from the cucumber farm. I floored the accelerator pedal again and rushed down the road. Less than ten minutes later, I reached the cucumber farm and luckily had no more police cars chase me down. I drove up to the gate and stopped. I rolled the window down and stared at the intercom, wondering what to do next. If Margot was already there, then no one would open the gate, and she'd know I was on her trail.

I decided I couldn't risk that, so I drove the truck to the gate instead, then got out, climbed into the back, and from there climbed the gate, then plopped down on the other side and began to run, praying I wasn't too late.

65

Panting and sweating in the moist night, I ran up the trail toward the farm. Rows and rows of cucumbers were on both sides of me, and soon I stood in front of the gray buildings where I had recently seen them prepare the cucumbers for leaving the farm. I stood for a few seconds and caught my breath, then ran around them and found the house behind them, where I had been drinking iced tea on the porch with Mrs. Cunningham just a few days ago. Despite the clammy heat, I shivered when thinking about my run-in with Mr. Cunningham and how he had yelled at me, telling me to get out of there.

I hurried to the front door, then decided to walk around the house and peek in the windows first to see what I was about to run into. In the driveway, a black Mercedes was parked, and I recognized it from Margot Addington's driveway. Standing on my tiptoes, I looked in through a window, and inside the living room, I spotted both of them. Mrs. Cunningham was sitting in a recliner while Margot Addington was standing in front of her, holding a gun.

Seeing this, I gasped and fell down with a loud thud. I lay still for a few seconds, fearing they might have heard me inside, then decided to get back up. I rose to my feet and walked out of the bush I had been standing in, then ran to the gray buildings and looked inside for anything I could use as a weapon. I found a shovel leaned up against a wall and decided that had to be it. I had no time to waste if I was going to get in there before Margot hurt Mrs. Cunningham.

With the shovel clutched between my hands, and nothing but my courage and hoping that luck was on my side, I stormed to the front door and poked it open, careful to not make a sound. I snuck inside and, as I did, Mrs. Cunningham spotted me, but I signaled for her to be quiet and I snuck up behind Margot, then lifted the shovel and swung it through the air, knocking her out so hard, she dropped the gun. I grabbed it and held it up in front of me.

"I am so sorry, Margot," I said. "But I had to do this."

Margot groaned from the tiles. Blood soaked her hair as she sat up, holding a hand to the wound. She looked up, closing one eye halfway in pain.

"What the heck? Rebekka Franck? What do you think you're doing?" she asked.

"Saving this town from any more killings and saving you from doing something you might regret for the rest of your life."

"It's a little late for that, don't you think?" she asked and grimaced in pain.

"If you're talking about your family, I believe you didn't want to harm them. You wanted to protect them from living a life where their mother and wife was stigmatized as a murderer. You wanted to end it all for both you and them. To spare them the pain. You never believed you would survive."

Margot sighed deeply, and then looked at Mrs. Cunningham, who stared at the gun in my hand.

"Give me that," she said and reached out her hand. "I'll call the sheriff."

"That might be a little hard, considering he's dead," I said. "He was killed a little earlier tonight."

Her eyes grew wide. "Leon? Dead? How?"

"That's actually what I thought you might tell me," I said and turned the gun to point it at her instead of Margot. "I think you have a lot of explaining to do, Mrs. Cunningham. Or are we close enough now for me to call you Bella?"

66

"It was when I read the article on Margot's table that it finally dawned on me," I said. "In the caption of the picture, it said *Mark Cunningham and his wife Isabella Cunningham, at their cucumber farm in Webster*. And that was when the dime finally dropped. I can't believe it took me so long. Bella Cunningham was Anna Mae Burke's best friend when growing up. You two were two peas in a pod, weren't you? At least according to your teacher. I've read through all the transcripts of the interviews that were made with Anna Mae back then and several others who were interviewed about her, among them, her teacher. And funnily enough, Anna Mae didn't even mention Bella's name once when she was interrogated, but her teacher did. She told the story of Bella and Anna Mae being inseparable, but also about how Bella was a little slow. That was why the police never brought you in for questioning, right? Because you couldn't help yourself; your mind wasn't completely there. Everyone knew it was so, but it was all an act, wasn't it? So people would never look in your direction. Meanwhile, you had Anna Mae so much under your control that she'd do anything for you, am I right? Even keep quiet when asked about the murders she had seen you commit. She'd even take the fall for you, am I right?"

I stared at Bella, then down at Margot, who was still holding a hand to her head.

"She told me she'd kill me too if I didn't," Margot said. "She was my best friend and the only one I had. I would do anything for her. So, I took the blame like she told me to. That was why she carved my initial on Benjamin Black's skin. To make sure I looked guilty. I let them think I had killed those two boys. I knew enough for them to suspect me. I had seen her commit both murders. I was there when she lured Timothy to come with us by telling him she had candy for him if he dared to go with her into the old abandoned house. All the kids in town were afraid of that house. No one dared to go in there except Bella. So, she told him he would get a lollipop if he did, and the kid fell for it. Then, once we were in there, she told him she believed he had a sore throat and told him she'd love to massage it for him. Then she grabbed him around the neck and started to rub her thumb against his skin. I had no idea what she was up to, and I just watched, thinking she was fooling around as usual. Then she started pressing, and I could tell the kid couldn't breathe. I told her to stop, but she wouldn't. Bella was freakishly strong and could beat me up any day, and she would. She would make me do all these things, like force a girl from our school to eat sand. It was all her idea; I just did as she told me. I shouldn't have, of course, but when you're ten years old, and the entire town already hates you because of your mother, you cherish the one friend you have. You don't say no to them; you don't risk losing them. I should have stopped her, I know I should have. So many times, while in prison, did I think about what I could have done, regretting just standing there in total apathy. I could have tackled her. I could have attacked her or thrown rocks at her. I could even have run for help, but the fact was, I didn't. And that makes me a murderer too. I felt like one and believed I deserved to go to jail. I was a weird child, and I was deeply fascinated with death, which later led me to write my novels. Back then, I had no idea how to act toward people because of my childhood, growing up with a mother who constantly tried to kill me or sell me to her clients, and the way I acted scared people. When I rang the doorbell of Mrs. Peterson's house, it wasn't to frighten them or even torment them. I wanted to pay my respects; I wanted them to know that the boy was missed, but it all came out the wrong way. And I was so interested in all aspects having to do with death that I wanted to see the boy again. It was strange; I can understand why they'd think that, but that's just how I was. They all thought I was being creepy and cruel, so they threw me away, and the town took it the wrong way. They decided I had to be the guilty one."

"They framed you, didn't they?" I asked. "The fibers. I went through the court files and noticed that the fibers weren't added till the very last day of the trial when the Chief Medical Examiner brought them in. He stated that they had been in the lab and that was why it took so long to get the answers, but no one had mentioned anything about carpet and sheet fibers being found on the bodies earlier on."

"I can't blame them," Margot said. "For thinking it was me. I knew where Benjamin Black's body was because I had helped Bella throw it into that well after doing the same to him as she did to Timothy. I wanted them to find him. That's why I made that drawing that led them to him. I had seen it all happen, and I had no idea how to tell the world. I had hoped my Aunt Carol would understand, that she would protect me, but I was wrong. She ended up giving them the fibers that they placed on the bodies. She was the one who really framed me."

"Along with Allan Cunningham and Leon Travers, am I right?" I asked. "They ganged up on you and gave the fibers to the Chief Medical Examiner, who made sure they became evidence overnight. He lied in court and said the fibers were found on the two boys' bodies when they were brought in, which they weren't. Now, the Chief Medical Examiner died ten years ago; I know since I have tried to locate him for my article, so we'll never get the truth from him. But the others could still have spoken. That's why they were killed, right?"

I turned to look at Margot, who nodded. Tears were now rolling quickly down her cheeks, and she wiped them away. Bella stood like she was frozen.

"Twenty years of my life I spent in that hellhole," Margot said, crying. "Just because of you. And now I have lost everything once again because of you."

"What I don't get," I said pensively while realizing that Mark Cunningham had nothing to do with any of this like I had believed. It was all his wife's doing. He had just gotten angry at me because I had said that his son was murdered and not killed by accident. He just wanted to believe it was an accident, maybe because he too suspected that it wasn't?

"I don't understand who killed the sheriff and the old Cucumber King and then tried to frame me for it. At first, I was certain it had to be Margot because they were the ones who framed her, but now I realize she's no killer. You are the killer," I said and pointed at Bella. "You killed them, didn't you? To keep the truth from getting out? You knew that if it was somehow revealed that Anna Mae was framed, then chances were that people would soon begin to ask more questions, and at some point, you'd be exposed. That's why you decided to get rid of them, and probably Margot next. Am I right?"

I stared at Bella Cunningham, the gun vibrating in my hand. Margot looked at her too and had risen to her knees now. Bella smiled, then rose to her feet.

"Stop right there," I said. "Or I'll shoot you."

She chuckled, then shook her head. Then she looked like she was about to sit back down, but what Margot and I couldn't see was that she reached down next to her recliner and pulled out a shotgun, then pointed it at Margot's head, pressing it close. Then she reached out her hand toward me.

"Your gun, please, or she dies. She means nothing to me, remember that. As a matter of fact, I would be more than glad to see her go. She is kind of the only one left to tell what I did. I wouldn't mind wiping her off the face of the Earth."

Knowing she was right, I dropped the gun, then kicked it toward her. Bella picked it up and put it in her pocket, then she turned toward me and smiled.

67

"OH, MY, HOW THE TABLES HAVE TURNED, HUH?" BELLA said as I stared down the dark barrel of her gun. I was kneeling on the floor as she had told me to.

"To answer your question from earlier, no, you are not right. As a matter of fact, you couldn't be further from the truth."

Margot was kneeling behind me as I made sure to keep my body between her and Bella. The shotgun rested steadily in her hands, and she showed no sign of nervousness or even fear. My guess was a girl like her had been brought up shooting by her parents and holding a gun came naturally to her.

I glanced around for a weapon or something I could use as a shield. I couldn't run and leave Margot defenseless. Bella wouldn't hesitate to shoot her and then come after me, shooting me in the driveway or as I ran for the road. She could then call the police and tell them we had broken into her property and tried to kill her. They would believe her, and she might even be praised for having killed us both, especially me, whom they probably believed had killed both the Cucumber King and the sheriff. No one would question her explanation, and she'd get away with everything.

"What do you mean when you say I wasn't right?" I asked.

Bella leaned closer. "I mean that I didn't kill the sheriff or my father. Not that I didn't want to get rid of both of them, but it wasn't me."

"You're lying," I said. "Just like you lied to everyone back then."

"What do you know about anything?" Bella yelled and pressed the gun closer.

Margot whimpered behind me and cried. I wondered if I could somehow grab the gun, and get it out from between her hands, but realized it was too risky. My heart was pumping hard and my chest felt tight, making it hard to breathe.

What do I do?

"Please," I said. "I have children who need me to come home to them. No more people have to die today."

"You should have said that to Anna Mae before she came bursting in here holding a gun. She's the one who should have stayed away. She didn't have to come here in the first place."

"I just wanted you to tell the truth," Margot suddenly yelled from behind me. "I never meant to hurt you. I wanted you to admit to your guilt; I wanted my name cleared."

As she spoke, Margot rose to her feet. Sweat dripped down my back as I feared for what Margot was up to now.

"Margot," I said, "don't do anything stupid."

She shook her head. "No. No more. I am sick of keeping quiet. It's all I have done my entire life. I kept quiet about my mother and what she did to me; I kept quiet about Bella and what she had done. All because I was told not to say anything, but not anymore. You have taken everything from me. Shoot me if you will, Bella, but you can never bury the truth. It will surface anyway somehow."

Bella stared at her, then lifted the gun, so it pointed at Margot's head. "You're a fool, Anna Mae. You always have been. I'll make sure it's written on your tomb, Here Lies a Fool."

I stared up at Bella, who spat the last words out, holding the gun to Margot's head. I had a few precious seconds to try something, but what? Bella was a lot bigger than me and a heck of a lot stronger, but I had to at least try something. It was my last and only chance.

68

I KICKED BELLA'S KNEE WITH MY HEEL. HER KNEE collapsed, and the gun went off, the shot missing Margot above her head, then hitting the ceiling above us. Bella fell, nearly toppling on top of me. As she fumbled to regain her composure, I reached over and grabbed Margot's gun from Bella's pocket, then cocked it and fired while Bella lunged at me. The bullet grazed Bella's shoulder, ripping her shirt and a sending a mixture of blood, bone, and fabric into the air. Bella screamed in pain and was pushed backward. For one unforgiving second, I turned my head to see if Margot was all right when Bella lifted the shotgun toward my face and fired. I saw it happen because of Margot's reaction. As she saw the gun lifted, she leaped into the air, yelling, then landed on top of me, taking the bullet that was meant for me.

"MARGOT!"

She wasn't moving. She had landed face-first on the tiles, halfway on top of me, completely limp. The moment she landed on me, I dropped the gun, and it slid across the tiles, far away from my reach. I screamed and screamed while pushing Margot's body off myself. Meanwhile, Bella moved around, cursing under her breath. Blood was gushing from her wound, and I could tell she was in pain.

"Would you shut up?" she grumbled. "Shut up!"

I was paralyzed. I stared at the blood on my hands and couldn't stop screaming. Then, as I saw Bella get the shotgun ready once more, I reached over and kicked her in the face. Bella shrieked and fell backward, landing hard on the tiles. With a second kick, I managed to knock the gun out of her grip, and it went flying across the tiles and hit the wall behind her, out of her reach. Bella then lunged at me, and I kicked her till she flew back. But soon she came at me again, raising her fist in the air and letting punches rain down on me. As I fell backward, my face throbbing in pain, she went for the gun again, but I grabbed her by the ankle and pulled her back, then I climbed on top of her, held her down, then threw a punch, hitting her on the jaw so hard her head flew sideways and stayed there.

Panting, I stared down at her beneath me, making sure she didn't move, then went for Margot's gun. I rushed toward it and grabbed it between my fingers when I felt her hands on my shin, and I was pulled back forcefully. The gun was still in my hand, and as she pulled me closer, I managed to turn myself around and point it at her face.

She didn't seem to care and kept pulling at me, so I kicked her hard in the face instead, and she let go of me. I then scrambled to my feet, pushed through a sudden spurt of dizziness, then stood hovering above her, holding the gun between my hands, pointing it down at her.

She grunted and kicked my shin, and I bent forward in pain, then lifted the gun again and fired it, shooting her in the thigh. Bella screamed like an animal, then rolled to the side, while I stepped backward, panting and wheezing. I found my phone that had fallen out of my pocket during the fight, then dialed 911. Then I rushed to Margot's body and turned her on her side. She was still breathing, but only barely. The bullet had entered her back, and blood was gushing out. I pressed my hand into it, to try and stop the bleeding, but it didn't help much.

"Margot...I am so..."

"I...I...can't breathe," she sputtered, half choked.

"Just lay still," I said. "There's an ambulance on the way."

Tears filling my eyes, I stared into hers, seeing all the regrets and fears she had suffered, all the disappointments, all the injustice done to her.

"I...I had it all. For just a few seconds, I had it all," she whispered, struggling to get the words out.

"Stay calm, Margot," I said, grief already overwhelming me. "Please, just lie still; they're coming. They're on their way. You can make it, Margot, I know you can."

Her lips moved into almost a smile while her body jerked. "I...I don't want to. Let me go. I..." Blood sputtered out of her mouth, and I whimpered, then leaned close to her. Sirens were wailing in the distance.

"We got her," I said, trying to entice her to stay. "We got Bella, and the truth will finally be revealed. Please, stay here with us."

Margot's eyes were strained. She opened her mouth to speak. Blood sputtered out, and I felt like screaming.

"There's nothing...there's nothing for me here anymore. You get her for me; clear my name. She shot me in the back. It ends here for me," she said, then exhaled and never inhaled again.

"Margot? Margot?" I shrieked, then leaned over her, terrified. "NO!"

As I heard the ambulances rush up in the driveway and

the footsteps approach, I was certain I saw a smile spread across Margot's face.

69

"Let me get this straight; you're trying to tell me that you went into the sheriff's house and found him like that?"

Detective Carter, who had held me at the station all night, had narrow dark eyes and no hair. He was the type who had it all figured out already but just wanted me to confirm it, which I wasn't going to do. I wasn't going to admit to having killed Sheriff Travers, no matter how long they kept me.

"I found him on the couch, yes; a knife was stuck in his chest. And then he died while I tried to perform CPR on him. That's why I called the alarm central."

"And then, by chance, a few hours later, you were suddenly at the house where the woman whose father you are suspected of killing lives, along with Margot Addington, who we found dead, and Mrs. Cunningham who was mortally wounded?"

"It wasn't a fatal wound. I shot her in the thigh because she kept trying to kill me. She killed Margot. I've told you this a million times," I said, bone-tired.

We had been at it all night, going over the night's events again and again, and I was exhausted. I just wanted to sleep, at least for a few hours. Wasn't that a human right? I felt like the night's events became more and more of a blur, and I couldn't really keep the details straight, which wasn't to my advantage.

"Let's go back to the beginning. What were you doing at Sheriff Travers' house?"

I exhaled, then told him what I had said so many times before. "I had found something in the transcripts of the old case that I wanted to show him. I wanted to ask him about Isabella Cunningham's involvement in the killings of the two boys and why she wasn't questioned back then. I found out that Mrs. Cunningham was Bella when I saw the article on…"

"Margot Addington's table, yes," Detective Carter said with a sigh. "We've heard that. Okay, then let me ask you this, why did you kill Margot Addington? She is the only one who could have confirmed your story?"

"I didn't. Isabella Cunningham did. She wanted to shoot me, but Margot took the bullet for me. She saved my life."

"Nice little sob-story," Carter said and leaned forward. "If it were true. But we got another testimony from Isabella Cunningham. She says the both of you broke into her house and wanted to kill her because she knew that you had killed her father and Sheriff Travers. She said you shot Margot Addington when she said she didn't want to hurt her, when she didn't want to help you out anymore."

"That's nonsense. I'm sure your forensics will prove my story to be true," I said. "I didn't kill anyone. My hands were checked for residue. I never touched that shotgun. My hands would be covered in gunshot residue that matched the shotgun that killed Margot. They did find residue, yes, but that was from another gun. The one I used to shoot Isabella Cunningham with in self-defense. There will be no match with the shotgun on my hands."

Detective Carter's nostrils flared, and I could tell I had hit a soft spot. He knew I was right. If I had fired that gun, they would find the evidence all over my fingers. Now, they were going to find it on Isabella's instead. "We'll see about that. But several witnesses saw you run away from Sheriff Travers' house right before the police arrived. Why didn't you stay so you could tell your story? Running away makes you look guilty."

"First of all, I was the one who called for help; don't forget that. You have my voice on the recording. I ran away because I knew I would end up having to try and explain myself like I'm doing now. And I didn't have time for that because I had to stop Margot before...I thought she had killed Allan Cunningham and Sheriff Travers because of how they had framed her back then. I thought she was going for Isabella next because she too had been a big part of destroying her life. It would make sense, except she hadn't killed them. It wasn't her."

Detective Carter slammed his hand on the table. "Then who was it?"

"That's what I don't know," I said. I wanted to say Isabella Cunningham because she was the only person who I could see would benefit from seeing them dead, but I wasn't sure I believed it was her either. There was no chance that those two would ever reveal the truth since it would only hurt them both. The sheriff had gone to great lengths to cover for himself. He had lied about Alexander's death because he knew that, if he didn't, then people would know the killer was back, and that would mean it was the wrong person he had put away. It would mean the truth would come out about him framing Anna Mae.

But if Isabella Cunningham hadn't killed her father and the sheriff, then who had? Worse than that, an even bigger question still remained:

Who had killed Alexander?

70

I WAS PUT IN A CELL, WHERE I LAY DOWN ON A HARD BENCH for a few hours, finally able to get a little sleep. I didn't sleep very well, though. I kept waking up, gasping for air, bathed in sweat, crying loudly. I wrapped my arms around myself, trying to find comfort, then went back to sleep again, dreaming about my children.

As the morning came a few hours later, the door to my cell was opened, and a deputy stepped in.

"Your bail was posted. You can go but stay close. We'll have you in for more questioning later."

I sighed and got my few belongings from the lady behind the glass. My phone had died and needed to be charged before I could call Sune and let him know I was still alive. He was probably worried sick. Then I reminded myself that he wasn't my boyfriend anymore and that maybe he didn't really care that much anymore. The guard guided me out the door, where a woman with short curly hair and blue eyes stood waiting for me.

"You're the one who posted my bail?" I asked and approached her.

She nodded and held her purse close to her body, looking nervously around her.

"You're Adeline's friend?" I said.

The woman reached out her hand toward me. "I'm Carol."

"I remember you from the Farmer's Market. Did Adeline send you?" I asked.

She shook her head.

"I don't understand. Then why would you post my bail?"

She looked around. "Let's talk in the car. I'll take you back to your motel. I parked right over there."

I followed her to a green pick up truck and got in. Carol put the key in the ignition, and it roared to life. She left the parking lot behind the sheriff's station, and then rushed down the main street, looking like she believed all eyes were on her.

"So…care to explain? What's going on, Carol?" I asked. "I have a feeling you didn't do this out of the goodness of your heart."

She bit her lip and stopped at a red light. "You're right. I didn't. I'm Anna Mae's aunt. I was the only one in her life that actually knew what was going on with her at home. I was supposed to take care of her. I wanted to, and I tried to, but I failed. I failed miserably."

I stared at the old woman in the seat next to me. Her slightly slumped forward posture made her look smaller than she really was. She seemed like she was ten years older than Adeline, but my guess was that they were about the same age.

"I was the only one who could have helped when they started all those accusations, but instead, I let the fear overpower me; I let them get to me and, finally, I gave in."

"You helped them frame her," I said. "Margot told me

that. You gave them the fibers so they could plant them as evidence, didn't you?"

She nodded and took off as the light changed. "I was the only one she had. Her mother didn't want her; she tried to kill her, and when that didn't work, she used her and sold her to men who raped her. I let her live with me for a little while, but…you must believe me. I truly thought she had done those things. I feared she might hurt…more children. That's why I did what I did. That's why I helped them."

"But she was innocent," I said. "Isabella Cunningham killed those boys. She forced Anna Mae to keep quiet. Anna Mae saw her do it; that's why she knew so much about it; that's why it was easy to conclude that she was the one who had done it."

"I know that now," Carol said, then she took a turn down Second Street and drove past the old abandoned house. I shivered when thinking about Alexander being pulled out of it. "I read about it in the paper this morning. They say that the sheriff's office is looking into the old story and Isabella's involvement. They've reopened the case and are digging out all the old files and even looking into Sheriff's Travers' involvement."

"Really? They're actually doing that?" I said, feeling a light in the darkness. Apparently, Detective Carter had been listening to my story after all, much to my surprise. Maybe I had misjudged him entirely; maybe he wasn't as bad as I had assumed him to be.

"They said on the news earlier that it was because Anna Mae was shot in the back," she added. "Once they realized that, they decided to look into what you were telling them. Isabella kept telling them that she had shot an intruder and that she was within her rights, but the medical examiner said Margot, or Anna Mae, was shot in the back, which, apparently, is a whole different story. You're not allowed to shoot an intruder in the back because it can be argued that she didn't pose any danger. It's up to the jury, of course, but they say she risks being charged with murder."

My eyes grew wide. She had known. Margot had known when she took that last breath. *She shot me in the back*, were some of Margot's last words. That was why she had said it. She knew that Isabella could be charged with murder if she shot an intruder in the back. That was why she had smiled. By dying, she had finally gotten back at her old friend. She had finally gotten her revenge.

Carol drove into the parking lot in front of the motel, then stopped the truck. She turned to look at me.

"I feel awful for what I did to Anna Mae, and it will haunt me to the day I die. That's why I helped you. But that's not the only reason, I'm afraid. I need your help to find out who killed Sheriff Travers and Allan Cunningham because I have a feeling that whoever it was is coming for me next."

71

Carol walked me to my room, and I put in the keycard. I sighed, satisfied when opening the door. The motel room wasn't much, but it was way better than some prison cell. All I wanted was to jump into a shower while charging my phone, then get into bed and call my kids before hopefully getting a few hours of sleep. I was so tired that I saw black spots in front of my eyes.

"Will you be all right?" Carol asked. "If I leave you, will you be okay?"

I nodded and gave her a hug. "Thank you for getting me out. I don't know what I would have done if I had to spend another hour in there."

She nodded. "It was the least I could do. Now, get some sleep; you look like you need it."

I nodded, then held the slip with her number up that she had given me. "I'll call you later, and then we'll talk, once my mind is clearer again, and I can think straight."

Carol nodded. She lingered for a few seconds in the doorway, looking like she wanted something else from me.

"All right," I said. "Talk to you later, okay?"

Carol nodded. She turned around and walked down the corridor. I watched her as she approached her truck and got in, wondering if there was something Carol hadn't told me. It seemed like she had something she wanted to say to me but didn't quite dare to.

It'll have to wait, Rebekka. You need sleep.

I decided to ask about it later, then turned around to walk back to my door while Carol backed out, then took off. As I placed my foot on the threshold, I paused, then looked toward her truck as it left the parking lot and drove onto the street.

Then my eyes grew wide.

In the window in the back, I saw not one head poke up, but two.

Oh, dear God! Someone's in the truck with her! Someone must have crawled into the back seat and hidden there while she talked to me! I must warn her!

I searched for my phone, but as I pulled it out, I remembered it was dead. There was a phone in the room, and I ran to it, then dialed Carol's cell number that she had just given me.

"Pick up, pick up, come on, Carol."

When she didn't, I slammed the phone down, then ran into the street and looked after her truck. It had stopped at a red light further down and was taking off now. Heart pounding in my chest, I felt paralyzed with indecision.

Come on, Rebekka, think. Do something; think of something!

Not thinking straight, I walked right out in front of a pick-up truck, raising my hands in the air, signaling for it to stop. The truck came to a sudden halt.

"What are you doing?" the driver yelled. She peeked her head out, and I saw that it was Adeline.

"Thank God it's you," I said. "I need your help…"

"Don't you think you've done enough? The motel has

been crawling with police all night, and I just got my truck back from the police impound. I really don't think…"

I approached her. "It's Carol. She's in trouble."

Adeline stopped talking and looked up at me. She unlocked the doors by clicking a button.

"Get in."

72

WEBSTER, FLORIDA 1980

Carol waited outside the door until she was buzzed inside. Her heart was in her throat as she entered the room and sat down between the barren walls. It was her first time inside of a real prison, and it filled her with deep fear and a claustrophobic sense as she stared at the door in front of her, waiting for it to open.

She should have come sooner, she knew she ought to, but she simply couldn't get herself to come. It wasn't that she didn't want to see Anna Mae, she did, she missed her terribly, but she just felt so awful about what she had done.

The town had returned to normal, and people were mowing their lawns, trimming their palm trees, and greeting each other in the street like nothing had happened, like *it* never happened. Meanwhile, Carol sat on her porch and rocked in her chair, wondering how Anna Mae was coping inside that awful place.

They had put her in with the adults. Because of the seriousness of her crime, they had put her in with the worst murderers in the country. It made no sense to

Carol why they would go to such extremes for just a young girl.

Finally, the door swung open, and there she was. Her hands were chained together, and so were her feet, and she waddled like a penguin toward her aunt. Carol smiled when she saw her, a tear shaping in the corner of her eye, but Anna Mae wasn't smiling back. The light in her eyes was gone, and nothing but matte indifference was left in them.

"Anna Mae?" Carol said when she sat down in front of her. Her hair hadn't been washed in a long time and her bangs needed to be cut. They were falling down in front of her eyes. "How are you?"

Anna Mae glowered at her from behind the curtain of hair. The baby was rolled in and placed next to her, sleeping heavily in the crib. Anna Mae didn't seem to care and turned her face away.

Carol's eyes lit up, and she couldn't take them away from the sleeping child. "Can I see her? Can I hold her for just a second?"

Anna Mae shrugged. "I don't care."

Carol rose to her feet. She reached inside the bassinet and grabbed the tiny creature, then lifted her up in the air. Anna Mae didn't even look at the baby as Carol held her while smiling.

"Oh, dear Lord, she's gorgeous. What a beautiful little baby."

Carol held the girl in her arms and rocked her from side to side while staring at the small infant's face. The baby seemed to be smiling in her sleep, and the sight made Carol laugh.

"Oh, my, Anna Mae. She's the cutest thing. I can't believe how adorable she is. She looks just like you when you were that age."

Carol stared at Anna Mae, who refused to even look at the child. She had given birth to her less than three months ago at the hospital, and they had called Carol from the prison and told her about it. It had taken Carol this long to find the courage to come and see her.

"You can have her if you like her so much," Anna Mae grumbled. "Take her."

Carol's eyes grew wide. Had she heard right? "But… but Anna Mae? Certainly, she needs to be with her mother. You might be young, but you are the only parent she has."

"I don't want her," she said. "They're going to take her away anyway, so I might as well give her to you."

"But…but…I…" Carol stared at her niece. Anna Mae's eyes met hers, and she knew to stop arguing. Anna Mae rose to her feet and signaled to the guard that she wanted to go back. "Just make sure that I never see her again, or you for that matter."

73

ADELINE SURE KNEW HOW TO DRIVE. SHE RACED DOWN Market Boulevard and turned right, skidding sideways in the intersection where I had seen the red truck turn. Adeline stared, focused on the road ahead, her eyes completely fixated on the asphalt, then floored the accelerator once again as soon as the truck was back on the road.

"I see it; I can see her!" I yelled.

The truck took a left turn down a smaller road, and we followed, Adeline soon catching up to it. No one in the truck had realized we were following it yet, and it was just slowly driving down the road. I could still see two heads poking up inside of it through the back window.

"Get even closer," I yelled at Adeline. "As close as you can. We have to get all the way up to it, till you almost touch it."

She did the best she could, and I stared at the back of Carol's truck, taking a few seconds to breathe, and finding my courage.

"Now what?" Adeline asked. "What do we do?"

I rolled the window down, and the warm wind hit my face. "Now, we stop them."

"How?" Adeline asked, but by then I had already pulled half of my torso out of the window, and I couldn't hear her anymore. While the truck moved forward, I crawled onto its roof, and then slid down the hood, almost going too far, shrieking, then managing to stop myself at the front. Then, as soon as Adeline came close enough, I leaped onto the back of Carol's truck. Unfortunately, she sped up right in that instant, and the back was suddenly farther away than what I had calculated. I managed to grab onto the edge of it and hang there, slamming my face against the tailgate, clinging on by only the tips of my fingers. Adeline then drove her own truck really close, and I managed to step onto the grille, and using it as my stepping stone, using all the strength I had in my poor arms, I pulled myself over and landed in the back of Carol's truck.

74

Carol felt the cold knife scraping the skin on her throat. Sweat was springing to her upper lip, and her hands were getting clammy, even though they were driving with all the windows down since the AC didn't work.

"Turn left here," the voice behind her said.

"Please," Carol said. "It doesn't have to end like this."

"Except it does," the voice said. "And you know it. You ruined my mother's life, and now I am going to take yours. It's as simple as that."

"But…but…"

"Take the left here now," she growled and pressed the knife closer to Carol's skin.

Carol turned the wheel, and the truck skidded sideways.

"W-where are we going?" she asked.

"You'll see."

Carol cried. The salty tears rolled down her cheeks and landed on her lips. "I'm sorry," she said. "You have no idea how sorry I am and have been for all of my life."

"It's a little late for that, don't you think?" the voice said.

A loud thud made them both gasp.

"What was that?" the voice said and turned her head to look behind her.

Carol looked in the mirrors and thought she spotted someone in the side view mirror. She was certain she saw hair blowing in the wind and maybe the top of a head.

What the heck is going on?

Her kidnapper was still staring behind her, looking out through the window, but didn't seem to be able to see anything, so Carol pretended like she hadn't either.

"We ran over a bump back there," Carol said. "Suspension isn't the best on this old truck."

The woman with the knife turned her head back toward Carol. "Go faster. I think that green truck back there is following us."

Carol looked in the mirror again and spotted Adeline's old truck. Her heart raced in her chest. What was she up to? Did she somehow know what was going on?"

The woman recognized the truck too now and became upset. "What the heck…Adeline? Why is Adeline following us, huh? Did you somehow tell her?" the woman said and pressed the knife against Carol's throat, so it felt like it cut into her skin.

Carol swallowed and did her best not to freak out. She had to keep her cool now and figure out what to do.

"Take a right down here and then lose Adeline. This truck is way faster than her old one."

Carol nodded, took the turn, and sped up as instructed, not daring to do otherwise. She was getting worried about Adeline and that she might get caught up in all this.

"It would be easier if you'd just tell me where we're going," Carol said.

"We're going to the old lot, the one where Benjamin Black was found. There's a well out there where I can dispose of your body. I thought there was a nice irony to it."

"They'll come for you, and they'll lock you up," Carol said. "Do you want that?"

"Do you think I care about my life, huh? I was doomed from the beginning. Born in prison to a woman who never wanted me. For years, I hated her because I believed she had simply abandoned me, but now that I know her true story, I realize that she was the victim here. She was the victim of your betrayal and of this entire town's betrayal. You didn't just destroy her life when you did what you did; you destroyed mine as well. I grew up thinking I was incapable of love, that no one would ever love me, not even my own mother. I knew I had been cheated of what I was supposed to have, a life of luxury, but instead, I had to live with the fact that I was the daughter of a murderer. Do you know how many nights I have lain awake wondering if I would become like her? Wondering if I had it in me to kill someone? And then now…finding out that it was all a lie? That she was innocent?"

Carol looked at her in the rearview mirror, when she thought she saw movement in the side view mirror again but pretended like she didn't.

A second later, she saw more movement, this time an entire body slinging itself in through the open window. Carol's eyes left the road as she looked in the mirror and saw legs swinging through the cabin and knocking into the face of the woman in her back seat. The woman screamed, and the knife was quickly removed from her throat, slicing the skin off as it slid back, cutting just deep enough to open her neck for a bloodbath.

Blood gushed out, and Carol screamed, then grasped

her throat. In the back, the two were fighting, while Carol felt the Earth start to spin around her. Soon, she could no longer keep her eyes on the road or her hands on the wheel.

75

"CAROL!"

Carol went quiet and slumped down in her seat. I was on top of the woman, who was fighting me while holding a bloody knife in her hand when the truck suddenly started to turn sideways. I held the woman down, holding her arms, and that was when I finally saw who it was. The realization blew out all the air from my lungs.

"Regina?"

I held her down, staring surprised at her face while the shock took root; I tried to force the knife out of her hand. Regina somehow managed to get enough room to knee me in the stomach, and I yelped. Meanwhile, the truck was driving off the road now and bumping down the grass toward a swampy area. I saw trees approaching in the distance, while Regina got her hand free and pushed me down, the knife in her hand getting scarily close to my throat. I grabbed her wrist and tried to fight the hand with the knife in it, trying to hold it back, my hand shaking as she groaned and pressed down on it.

The truck hit a bump and Regina flew against the ceiling. As she did, I managed to get out from underneath her, and as soon as she landed again, I punched her in the face, hard, knocking her out. Then I took the knife and turned to look out the windshield, where I spotted the row of trees right in front of us.

I sprang to the front seat, grabbed the wheel, then turned the truck sideways forcefully. It skidded, then slammed into the trees on the side and I was knocked unconscious in the process, the knife flying out of my hand and landing on the floor.

When I woke up, I saw Adeline in the open door. She was pulling Carol out, her face torn in fear. Carol landed in the grass and Adeline tried to stop the bleeding using her shirt that she had ripped.

I blinked my eyes, and as soon as I could see straight, I rushed out to them.

"She's lost a lot of blood," I said and looked at the front seat of the truck that was completely soaked in her blood.

"I called for help," Adeline said. "I just hope they'll make it in time. I saw…through the window…I saw who it was."

I nodded, sensing the deep despair in Adeline's voice.

"Keep applying pressure," I said. "She'll make it."

"She's the one who gave me Regina, did you know that?" Adeline said, sobbing. "She was Anna Mae's child, but she gave her to Carol, who realized she couldn't keep her. She wanted Regina to grow up in a home where the mother didn't look at her and think she might grow up to become a murderer. After having Anna Mae in her house, she didn't dare to have Regina. She wanted her to grow up out of her mother's shadow. So, she gave her to me, and I loved her like she was my own. I can't believe what she has done. Why would she try and kill her?"

"Anna Mae is…" I mumbled to myself. "That's what

the sheriff said right before he died. He wasn't trying to say *Anna Mae is innocent* like I believed he was. It wasn't three words. What he was trying to say was *Anna Mae's…daughter*. He was trying to tell me who had killed him."

Adeline looked at me, her eyes stricken with sadness and fear. "I tried my best to raise her right; where did I go wrong? How could I…"

Adeline paused mid-sentence, then stopped. I hadn't seen it happen until it was too late, and I barely had a chance to react before I saw Regina standing behind her, and the knife had already been plunged into Adeline's back. Adeline gasped, then bent forward, the knife still in her. Regina was still holding onto the handle, then she applied pressure to it, pushing it in further.

"You couldn't, dear Mother," she said. "There was nothing you could have done. I was the daughter of a murderer, remember? I knew I would grow up to be one too. It was inevitable. It was just a matter of time."

I stared at Adeline, barely able to breathe properly, paralyzed by shock. Regina pulled the knife out of her mother's back, and Adeline's lifeless body fell forward on top of Carol. I shrieked and pulled back, while Regina stared at the bloody knife.

"He had my life, you know? Alexander Cunningham did. That was why I killed him. I wanted to know what it felt like to be like my mother, and he was the perfect toy to try it on. All my life, I had fought my desire to try it, but as I saw him that day sitting in his car all alone, I stopped fighting it and just gave in. I knocked on the window, and he opened the door for me. I told him to come with me, told him I had seen something exciting inside the old house, and I wanted to show him. He didn't dare to, he didn't want to go with me, but I told him it would make him tough in the other kids' eyes, that they would be very impressed that he dared to go inside of the old house, and he fell for it. He took my hand and walked inside with me, and in there, as soon as the door had closed behind us, I told him to stand still and let me look at his throat. I asked him if it was sore, and if he wanted me to massage it. He nodded, and I did. I placed my fingers on his throat and pressed. I strangled him with my bare hands. It doesn't take much pressure to a small boy's throat to kill him like that. I almost didn't put enough pressure on it to block his airways, and he didn't even fight me. His eyes just rolled back in his head, and he died right there in my arms. I returned a few days later to paint my message on the wall like my mother had done at the nursery. I wanted them to think she was back. I wanted to scare them."

I stared at Regina and the knife in her hands, not knowing what to do. I felt completely destroyed by what she had done to Adeline.

"Why? Why do you s-say that he had your life? Wait a minute, was…did…Allan Cunningham was your…?"

"My father, yes. He was a regular at my grandmother's house, and every now and then, she'd sell my mother to him. She didn't know the girl had developed early and had already had her first period since she had been hiding it from her. The last time it happened, dear Aunt Carol walked in on them and saw it. That was when she took Anna Mae in, but it was too late. She was already pregnant. That was why Allan Cunningham was so eager to get her locked away. She held the power to destroy him in her belly. Me. Carol told me the story when I was a teenager and began asking about my birth parents. To think that she ganged up with him to get my mother put away, him of all people, disgusts me. And then the deputy who was so certain of her guilt that he'd do anything because he loved his godson so much. Guess love can make you do terrible things too, huh? Not just hatred. Now, when I killed the boy, the sheriff, and daddy dearest, I felt nothing but hatred for them. All my life, I had believed my mom was a murderer, and then I find out that she was framed? Forty years later, it is revealed that it was actually someone else who killed those boys and that these three were to blame for what happened to her? I had to get revenge for her because I knew she wouldn't do it herself. And now she's gone. I never even got to know her. She was right there, living right outside of town, less than ten minutes away, and I didn't even know. I can't help but wonder why she never looked for me."

"Maybe she was afraid of what she might find," I said. In the distance, I could hear sirens blaring. It was the sound of help approaching. All I had to do was to keep her talking, keep her occupied till they arrived. But it was easier said than done. Regina heard the sirens too and lifted her head to look me straight in the eyes. She held up the knife, a range of desperation rushing over her face as she realized they were closing in on her.

Then she turned around and took off in a run.

"Oh, no, you don't," I exclaimed, then rose to my feet as fast as I could and lunged at her. I grabbed her by the legs, and she fell face-first flat in the grass. She groaned and kicked me in the face again and again, till I had to let go of her legs. She wiggled herself out of my grip while I moaned in pain. She got up again and took off, but I was faster. I jumped her from the back and took her down again, then landed on top of her. We rolled around and threw punches, then the sirens came closer, and I could hear them stop. Then there were voices yelling while I lay on top of Regina, holding her down with all my weight.

"Over here!" I yelled. "I've got her! HELP!" I screamed

at the top of my lungs. Seconds later, I heard voices approach.

"Over here. POLICE! STOP!"

I held her down the best I could while she squirmed underneath me, and I didn't even feel the blade of the knife before it had plunged through my abdomen.

76

I heard my children's voices through the fog and tried to run toward the sound, but somehow, I wasn't moving no matter how much I tried.

"Julie? William? Tobias?" I screamed and looked around, but I couldn't find my way out of the dense fog. I was in a forest of some kind, and I had no idea how I had gotten there.

"Listen," I heard Julie say. "It's Mom. Mom? Are you there?"

The fog was closing in on me, and I couldn't see anything in front of me, not even my hand as I held it up. Panic set in. Where was my daughter? I could hear her but not see her; where was she?

"JULIE?"

"It is her," I heard her say. "She's awake. Mommy, are you awake?"

I was. I blinked my eyes a couple of times and the fog disappeared slowly while I returned to the real world.

"Julie?" I said, staring into the beautiful eyes of my

daughter. I laughed, but it hurt, so I stopped. I tried to lift my head, but I couldn't.

"Don't try to get up," Sune said, coming up behind Julie. His eyes were red-rimmed. "You're hurt. Badly."

"Mommy?" William poked his head up next to my bed. Never had I seen a dearer sight. Tears ran down my cheeks as I looked at him. "She's awake, Daddy. Now, you don't have to cry anymore."

I looked up at him, then sent him a cautious smile. He looked away and wiped his eyes.

"Yeah, well…"

"Will you be okay?" Tobias asked. He was standing on the other side of the bed, keeping a little bit of distance. I reached out my hand and pulled him closer.

"The doctors didn't think you'd make it," Julie said. "That's what they told Sune."

"Really?" I asked. "Guess I proved them wrong, huh?"

"You were gone for a very long time there, Rebekka," Sune said. "We were all terrified. You've been out for a week. They said you lost a lot of blood and that they weren't sure you'd come back to us. But it isn't over yet. The knife went through your kidneys and damaged both of them. You'll need a transplant as soon as possible, or you'll die."

"Oh," I said and looked down at the tubes and bandages.

Sune rubbed his hair distraughtly. "Yeah, well, apparently I'm a match, so…"

I stared at him, not sure I was hearing him right. "Say that again?"

He threw out his arms. "I'm giving you my kidney."

"Oh, Sune, you don't have to…"

He smiled, a tear escaping his eye. "Don't you get it? I want to. I have treated you awful, and it's the least I can do. Besides, you're the mother of my child. I need you to stick around. We all do."

I was crying now while looking into his eyes. I couldn't believe he would do this for me.

"I am not taking your kidney, Sune. I can't do it. There must be another way? Some other donor?" I asked, sobbing.

Julie tried to hug me, but the tubes got in her way. Instead, I held her hand in mine, and she put her forehead against mine.

"I love you, Mom."

"I love you too, sweetie."

She was crying now and not even trying to hold it back anymore. "I don't know what I would do if you hadn't come back. I was so scared."

"I would never leave you, baby. Never."

She looked deep into my eyes, then stroked my cheek gently. "So, please, take Sune's kidney, will you? For my sake. For all of us."

Sune grabbed my hand in his. "I know you hate me for what I have done, and we won't be together anymore; I've come to terms with that now, but at least let me save your life. We're lost without you, Rebekka."

77

I SAT ON THE EDGE OF THE BED WHILE PUTTING ON MY clothes very carefully. The nurse who had been taking care of me for the entire two weeks I had been in the hospital after the transplant helped me get them on and supported me while I put them on properly.

I could still barely stand on my own, and they rolled in a wheelchair for me to sit in.

Sune poked his head in, flanked by all three children. "You ready to go?"

I nodded, and the nurse placed my bag in my lap. She smiled at me.

"Now, you keep yourself out of trouble, okay? I don't want to see you in here again except for your check-ups. If you have any pain or if you don't have urine, then let us know, okay?"

It had taken three days for the kidney to start working, and I had been so scared my body would reject it or that it simply didn't fit somehow. But the doctor had explained to me that it was normal. He said that a good transplant was one that worked well after a year and not two weeks. Meanwhile, they had put me on dialysis till it started working on its own. I would have to come back for check-ups two to three times a week, to begin with, then once a week, then once every two weeks. When they were finally satisfied that it worked well, the appointments would be reduced to once every three months, but that was a long way off. For now, I was going to have to accept help for a long while, and Sune and the kids had promised to take good care of me.

I hugged the nurse and thanked her for being so good to me, then let Sune push me in the chair toward the eleva-tor. I couldn't wait to leave this place and get out in the fresh air and feel the sun on my face again.

"Were you going to leave without even saying goodbye?"

I turned my head and spotted Carol standing in the doorway of her room. She was holding her IV drip in her hand, rolling it behind her. She still had a huge bandage on her throat and was pale from the loss of blood. They had managed to stitch her back together again, but it had been a close call, they said.

"Of course not," I said and reached out my hand toward her. She bent down and hugged me.

"I am so sorry about Adeline," I said, my voice growing hoarse. "It wasn't fair."

Carol nodded, her eyes growing wet. "She was a good woman. I will miss her terribly."

"We should go now," Sune said from behind me as the elevator dinged its arrival. "William needs to get his nap."

I stared at my tired son, then chuckled. "He'll sleep in the car."

"See you at the trial," Carol said and waved at me as

269

Sune rolled me into the elevator. "Maybe we can grab lunch?"

"Sounds awesome," I said, not looking forward to having to face Regina again in a courtroom, but also knowing it was necessary. She still claimed she was innocent and that she was being framed, but luckily, I don't think anyone believed her. She was, after all, found holding the knife that stabbed me and Carol and Adeline. Plus, they had also found her fingerprints on the knife that stabbed both Allan Cunningham and the sheriff, and they had found her hairs on Alexander Cunningham's clothes. She could cry innocence all she wanted, but I felt pretty convinced she'd go away for quite some time. It was still strange to me how she had wondered all her life if she was like her mother, if she too would turn into a murderer. It made me wonder about what you grew up knowing about yourself and if it was possible that you could somehow make those things come true, just by believing them about yourself. That how you saw yourself shaped you somehow.

We reached the lobby and Sune pushed me out through the sliding doors, where I took in a deep breath of the warm moist Florida air that I had grown to love so dearly.

"It's funny, life," Sune said as he pushed me toward the car in the parking lot.

"What is?" I asked.

"It's kind of ironic that you were recently pushing me around, helping me with even the smallest things like going to the bathroom, and now I'll be doing the same for you."

"I fail to see what's so funny about that," I said and looked up at him. He smiled.

"At least I know how it feels to be in your situation," he said.

"And I know how you feel," I said.

Sune smiled again. "Plus, I kind of like the feeling that you'll always carry a small part of me with you wherever you go for the rest of your life. You'll never get rid of me completely."

"Another example of life's cruel irony, I guess," I said and let him help me into the passenger seat of the car.

EPILOGUE

"CAN SOMEONE GET THAT?"

I was sitting in the living room in my wheelchair when the knock came on our door. I looked around. No one was there to open the door. Sune had left for Publix to buy groceries and taken William with him, while Julie and Tobias had taken their boogie boards down to the beach.

"Dang it," I said, then grabbed the wheels of my chair. I pulled them when there was another knock. I still wasn't very good at wheeling this thing since I had only been at it for three days. I wasn't sure I was ever going to get good at it. I had blisters on my fingers from trying, and to be honest, I was hoping to lose it soon. The hospital had believed it was best for me not to move around too much, so they had said at least a week in the chair, to make sure the scars from the operation would heal properly and not to risk ripping out the stitches from where the knife went through.

"I'm coming; I'm coming, geez," I said and fought to roll the chair across the tiles. I reached the door, finally,

272

then panting tiredly, I reached for the handle and turned it. I opened the door, expecting it to be the mailman or a FedEx delivery guy wanting a signature, but it wasn't. What met me on the other side made me first think that I had to be dreaming.

"David? David Busck?"

David's handsome eyes stared at me. Was it possible that he was even dreamier than the last time I had seen him?

David was a journalist like me, and that wasn't the only thing we had in common. David and I had been stuck in a limestone mine some years back, and he had come to my town afterward and told me he cared deeply for me. I had almost fallen for him back then while Sune and I were apart for a little while, but then I decided to stay with Sune after he was shot.

"It's good to see you, Rebekka. It's been awhile."

"What on Earth…why are you here?" I asked. "In Florida of all places?"

"I was on a job here, actually all the way in North Carolina, doing a story about a group of ex-soldiers who have made this small community, living in the woods, struggling with their PTSD, completely cutting themselves off from society. I write for a psychology magazine now, and it was quite interesting, actually. Anyway, I was there and spent a couple of weeks living with these guys, and then when I came back to civilization, I heard about what happened to you. Your name was on the news up there with a picture and everything. I decided to track you down."

I wrinkled my forehead, then looked down at my wheelchair. I hadn't showered in two days, and my hair was greasy. I wasn't exactly the woman I used to be.

"I can't believe it," I said and let him hug me, even though I knew the smell couldn't be good. "How long are you here?"

He shrugged. "I don't know yet. As I was doing my story up north, I came upon another one that I might be looking into that is pretty close to here in Orlando. I thought I might stick around for a few weeks. See what the fuss about this state is all about."

I felt baffled and slightly puzzled as well. I hadn't forgotten about David, but I had pushed him out of my mind and thought I'd never see him again. Yet there he was, looking at me the same way he had back then.

"Okay, if I'm going to be perfectly honest," he continued, "I ran into your father before I left, and he told me that you and Sune had split up but that you were still staying here, at least for a little while. I was coming here anyway and was hoping I'd find you. Then this story was all over the news, and well…I got worried about you, and feared that you were all alone."

"Well, I'm not. Sune has been taking care of me. And the kids of course."

"But…? Please let there be a but?"

"But we're not together anymore," I said. "He's seeing someone else."

"And you?"

"I am mostly seeing the TV lately."

David smiled. "So, would that mean that…if I stayed in town, that maybe I could take you out to dinner sometimes?"

I looked down at the wheelchair, then decided it didn't matter. David had seen me at my worst when being stuck together in that mine. Besides, I was only attached to this thing for a short while. I was soon going to be back to myself, or a stitched-up version of me, at least.

I nodded with a smile.
"I would really like that."

THE END

AFTERWORD

Dear Reader,

Thank you for purchasing *It Ends Here* (Rebekka Franck #10). A big part of this story is inspired by real events. A girl named Mary Bell killed two boys in England back in 1968 together with her friend. She was later convicted of these murders and served 12 years in prison. When she was released, she gained court-ordered protection of her identity so she could start a new life, but it was revealed who she was later on and her daughter learned the truth about her mother in 1998 when the house was besieged by the media. After that, it was ruled by a judge that the press was banned from writing anything that could reveal her identity. The judge then said: "We don't want to visit the sins of the mother on the child." I found that to be an interesting statement, which grew to be the foundation of this book.

I then combined her story with the story of an author who had also been convicted of a murder when she was a child, and her identity was exposed when they suddenly made the movie called *Heavenly Creatures* about her. She had changed her name and moved to another part of the world, but it still caught up with her, which I also found to be very interesting.

If you want to know more, you can read about both stories here:

https://en.wikipedia.org/wiki/Mary_Bell

https://www.heraldscotland.com/news/12296872.mary-bells-daughter-learns-the-awful-truth-court-move-to-protect-identity/

https://www.theguardian.com/books/2003/nov/12/crimebooks.features11

Now, the town of Webster does exist and is a small town here in Florida. The Farmer's Market also exists and is actually worthy of a visit, especially on cattle-auction days. The restaurant has a great atmosphere and serves typical southern country-style food. Some of the other places I have written about exist as well, like the Circle K outside of town and the stores, but I have also taken the artistic liberty to move some things around in the town, and none of the characters in this book are based on living characters from this town.

As always, I want to thank you for supporting me and remind you to leave a review if you can. It means so much to me.

Take care,

Willow

To be the first to hear about new releases and bargains—from Willow Rose—sign up below to be on the VIP List. (I promise not to share your email with anyone else, and I won't clutter your inbox.)

- Sign up to be on the VIP LIST here:
http://readerlinks.com/l/415254

Tired of too many emails? Text the word: "willowrose" to 31996 to sign up to Willow's VIP text List to get a text alert with news about New Releases, Giveaways, Bargains and Free books from Willow.

Follow Willow Rose on BookBub here:
https://www.bookbub.com/authors/willow-rose

Follow Willow Rose on Amazon here:
https://readerlinks.com/l/160860

Connect with Willow online:
https://www.facebook.com/willowredrose
www.willow-rose.net
http://www.goodreads.com/author/show/
4804769.Willow_Rose
https://twitter.com/madamwillowrose
madamewillowrose@gmail.com

ABOUT THE AUTHOR

 The Queen of Scream, Willow Rose, is an international best-selling author. She writes Mystery/Suspense/Horror, Paranormal Romance and Fantasy. She is inspired by authors like James Patterson, Agatha Christie, Stephen King, Anne Rice, and Isabel Allende. She lives on Florida's Space Coast with her husband and two daughters. When she is not writing or reading, you'll find her surfing and watching the dolphins play in the waves of the Atlantic Ocean. She has sold more than three million books.

To be the first to hear about new releases and bargains—from Willow Rose—sign up below to be on the VIP List. (I promise not to share your email with anyone else, and I won't clutter your inbox.)

- SIGN UP TO BE ON THE VIP LIST HERE :
http://readerlinks.com/l/415254

Tired of too many emails? Text the word: "willowrose" to 31996 to sign up to Willow's VIP text List to get a text alert with news about New Releases, Giveaways, Bargains and Free books from Willow.

ITSY BITSY SPIDER

EXCERPT

For a special sneak peak of Willow Rose's Bestselling Mystery Novel ***ITSY BITSY SPIDER*** turn to the next page.

PROLOGUE

1977

At first she thought it was an accident that the door to the bunker had shut. Then she tried to open it on her own, but couldn't. It was either too heavy or it must have locked when it shut. She knocked carefully.

"Hello?"

The quiet coming from outside the iron door was almost cruel. Astrid swallowed and knocked once again, this time harder.

"Hello?"

But nothing. Nothing but the horrendous sound of her own breathing. *Someone will open it. Once they realize it has shut, they'll come.* Astrid took the few steps from the door down into the bunker. She felt tired and her feet were swollen. She sighed and sat down on a bench, waiting, staring at the door, and anticipating it swinging open at any moment now. Except, it was actually two doors, separated by a small hallway between them. So even if she hammered, they wouldn't be able to hear her. All she could do was wait. Someone would eventually come for her.

Wouldn't they? Of course they would. He would come. He who told her he loved her…

Astrid knew she wasn't among the smartest of the young kids on the island. Her mother always told her that. But Astrid had good hands and she wasn't a half-bad cook. If she stuck to what she knew, she might be lucky enough to one day have a man, her mother had promised. Now Astrid had found one. And he wanted more than just her cooking. He wanted her. He loved her, he said. Then he made love to her in the dunes by the beach.

He was nice to her and she wanted him to meet her mother, but he kept telling her: *not now, not today.* Astrid never thought of asking when. She just waited patiently for him to find the time in his busy schedule. She never wondered why he never took her places, or why he insisted they only meet at night, or why he never spoke to her except for the dirty words he whispered in her ears; Astrid was educated enough to know that these words weren't something they would say in church.

No, Astrid never thought there could be anything wrong with her relationship with this boy who once said he loved her, and who showed his love for her in the dunes again and again, night after night, during that endless summer in 1977. Instead, she started looking forward to their life together, preparing herself to one day become his wife, and to have a baby.

"You'll get nothing but dummies like yourself," her mother had said. "There should be a law that demanded that people like you were sterilized so you wouldn't pass your stupidity on to your kids. Stupid girl," she said, and slapped Astrid across the face.

Yes, Astrid was very well aware that she wasn't the smartest among people, but she had a good heart. That much she knew. One day she would become a great mother to a child who would have its father's intellect, and that child was going to go out into the world and do great things.

"That'll show them," she said, sniffling, while staring at the closed iron door at the top of the stairs.

"He'll come for me, won't he?" she asked, and her voice echoed into the small room behind her that was lit only by a lightbulb hanging from under the ceiling. *Of course he will. Of course.*

Astrid drew in a deep sigh. She looked around and spotted the big flashlight on a shelf in the corner among blankets, water bottles, and canned food. She pulled the flashlight out and held it in her hand. Then she sat down again, waiting for someone to come and get her. *Not just someone. Him, the boy of her dreams, the love of her life. Not just anyone.*

Astrid sighed and calmed herself down. She always did this, her mother would say; she always made herself uneasy or even anxious for no reason at all.

1

2012

THE MAN WAS LOOKING IN THE WINDOWS OF THE FRENCH doors leading into the kitchen. It was dark inside the mansion by the ocean. A small light under the door revealed that there was someone in the other room next to the kitchen. Just as he had hoped.

The man lifted his gloved hand and smashed it through the small window, then reached through and unlocked the door. He opened it without making any sound at all. Smoothly, he slid through the door and into the woman's kitchen. Carefully, he closed the door behind him, while stepping on the broken glass strewn underneath his heavy boots.

The man turned and looked at the perfect kitchen. Knives were hanging on the wall. He grabbed one and looked at it in the moonlight that poured into the room. Then he sighed with a deep feeling of satisfaction while putting it back. He reached into his own sports bag and found his own set of knives rolled up in their bag. Like a professional chef, he unfolded the bag and rolled the knives out on the table.

What a beautiful sight to his eyes. Clean blades, sharpened to perfection. Almost a pity he had to mess them up. Cutting through meat and bones always made them dull. The man picked one out and put the rest back in his bag. Then he approached the door leading to the adjacent room, where he could tell the TV was on.

The man had studied the woman's daily routine for weeks now and knew she always dozed off to her favorite show, *The Sopranos*, before she awoke and went to the bathroom at exactly ten-thirty. She was as precise as a clock. Then she would go into the kitchen and grab a glass of water to put next to her bed for the night. She seemed to have a hard time sleeping lately and he speculated that this made her thirsty.

The man walked out of the kitchen door and into the hallway as he heard the theme song for *The Sopranos*, and then the TV went silent.

The man sat down on a chair in the corner of the guest bedroom and waited, listening to the woman performing her routines, like he had done many times before, but this time was different. This was the big finish, *le grand finale*, as they said in French.

The man glanced at his reflection in the mirror on the dresser. He touched his pale skin and followed one of the veins with his finger. Then he smiled at himself. He had been looking forward to this moment for all of his life. He had prepared for it, dreamt about it, arranged it into details, just waiting for the right time and to be in the right place.

And the best of it? He was just starting out.

2

2012

Old Mrs. Heinrichsen let out a small shriek. The spider in her bathroom sink had startled her. They always did. She shook her head and turned on the tap. The spider tried to fight the river of water, clinging on to the slippery side as the water was threatening to flush it down the drain. Mrs. Heinrichsen watched its struggle with great joy and turned the tap to speed up the water. She grinned and sang while watching the spider fight for its life.

> *"The Itsy Bitsy Spider crawled up the water spout.*
> *Down came the rain, and washed the spider out.*
> *Out came the sun, and dried up all the rain,*
> *And the Itsy Bitsy Spider went up the spout again."*

Finally, the spider gave up, lost the fight, and disappeared with the water into the drain. The old woman liked these small displays of power over nature. She had always enjoyed them over humans as well, but in recent years, respect for her and her status on the small island had diminished. No one seemed to care who she was or who she had been anymore.

There was a time when it wasn't only spiders that had struggled to stay alive by her mercy. Oh, how she missed those days. How she missed seeing the fear and terror in people's eyes as she drove down the street in her new car, or went for a stroll showing off her newest fur brought in from Paris, or a new jumpsuit from Milan. Those were the days. Those were the times she had cherished and would remember as her golden years.

But these days, no one cared anymore. No one respected her in the manner they had back then. To them, she was just an old lady. Someone whose time was ticking down. Someone who was close to the finish line of life. The youngsters of today didn't have any respect for status or title anymore. It was all just the same baloney to them. They didn't care about her position; hell, most of them hardly knew her name anymore.

Mrs. Heinrichsen finished brushing her teeth and walked back towards the bedroom. The old wooden floors of her villa creaked underneath her weight, even though she could hardly make it past ninety pounds anymore. She was still a strong woman and she expected to live at least twenty years more.

"Gotta make it past the one hundred mark," she always said. "Get the letter from the queen before you go."

It was her goal, and Mrs. Heinrichsen always reached her goals. This was something she had tried to teach her son, but in vain. Today, people didn't seem to care about setting goals and reaching them, or about doing what it took to make it, no matter what the cost. Working to accomplish something. Nowadays it was all about how to get out of working and how to get the state to pay for everything. She saw people like this down by the harbor, down by the boats leading to the mainland. These people who could just as well be working, but here they were instead, drinking their beers, hanging out with their dogs, and sporting dirty clothes. Mrs. Heinrichsen knew they got paid from the state to live that kind of life. Destitute was the nice word for them. People who couldn't take care of themselves, so the state had to step in. Freeloaders, Mrs. Heinrichsen would call them. In her book, they were nothing but people who didn't want to work. And lately, with all those newcomers, all those brown people who had almost invaded the country, even their small island, and were all being paid huge amounts from the state to get all their relatives up here, it was about to destroy the small paradise, destroy Denmark with all their demands, under the pretense that they just wanted to be *equal*. How those dirty faces could ever get the thought that they were equal to the proud hardworking Danish people, she never understood. It was an atrocity. The beautiful country had been invaded by these…these foreigners…and Mrs. Heinrichsen certainly didn't like what they were turning this country into.

Mrs. Heinrichsen entered her bedroom and sat on her bed wearily. It had become increasingly difficult for her to lie down with her breathing troubles, and she wasn't looking forward to yet another night sitting up and sleeping. The nights had become long and painful to her lately and even though she did take a small nightcap, it never quite helped her through the entire night.

"Oh, John. You bastard," she said, and looked at the empty side of the bed where he used to sleep. "I bet you're up there somewhere enjoying seeing me suffer through these nights, aren't you?"

The silence from the room was answer enough. Mrs. Heinrichsen leaned back on her stack of pillows and hugged her arms around her body. Barely had she closed her eyes before she heard a sound. Mrs. Heinrichsen got out of the bed again with much discomfort.

"If it's that neighbor's dog again, I'm sure I'm gonna…"

She never made it further than that. As she fought to get out of the bed and up onto her feet, she watched the door to her bedroom open quietly. Then she gasped.

A face appeared in the darkness.

"Hello, Agnes," the man said.

3

2012

"I can't believe you inherited a real house, Mommy."

I looked through the rearview mirror at my seven-year-old son, Victor, sitting in the back seat of our old Toyota. He was smiling and his small eyes sparkled. He had been so excited ever since we received the phone call telling me that my grandmother, my father's mother, had passed away, and much to my surprise, since I never knew her, that she had left her house to me.

My oldest child, my daughter Maya, was less excited, to put it mildly. But then again, at thirteen, not much was exciting, especially if it involved me, her mother, or anything remotely grown up and boring.

"Of course she inherited it, you doofus," Maya said to her younger brother. "She's her only grandchild."

"Well she could have left it to grandpa, her son," I argued, while finding my exit from the highway. "That would have been the most normal thing to do. But for some reason, she wanted me to have it."

"Why?" Maya asked with her lips curled, making her look like she was extremely annoyed.

I shrugged. "I don't know. I never even knew her. Grandpa says I met her once when I was just a small child, but I don't remember it. Maybe I chose to forget because she was too scary," I said, and made a funny face.

Maya looked mad. "You're so...so pathetic."

"Wow. Well, thanks."

That seemed to be the end of that conversation. It had been a long ride from Copenhagen to Esbjerg, and my children hadn't exactly been talking much. It was getting dark outside the car's windows and would be way past their bedtime by the time we arrived at our new house.

Victor had slept most of the way and Maya seemed to feel it was beneath her dignity to talk to me for more than three minutes at a time. She was pissed because I had made the decision for all of us. I had decided to move there, to my grandmother's house on Fanoe, a small island in the North Sea outside of Esbjerg. I knew it wouldn't be popular to make a decision like that on my children's behalf, but there was no way around it. I was broke and couldn't afford to keep our apartment in Copenhagen. I had been fired from my latest job as a writer for a fishing magazine, simply because I had pissed off the chairman of the Danish Fishing Federation, DFF, by asking him about the many bottles of expensive wine that the Federation had deducted on their taxes this year. Needless to say, it wasn't the kind of story that the magazine was looking for, so they kicked me out. Well, that's just the way things go. I wasn't exactly looking for a long-term career in fishing journalism anyway, but it had been a paying job, and it had allowed me to bring home enough money for the rent and expenses that my ex had left me with when he decided it was more fun to be with a twenty-five-year old intern at his TV station than to stay with his family.

"Are we there soon?" Victor asked with a slight whimper.

"Why?" I asked. "You need to go?"

Victor nodded heavily. "Badly."

Maya sighed and rolled her eyes. "You could have gone when we stopped for snacks."

"I did," Victor said.

"But that's only, like, ten minutes ago. How can you need to go already? We've stopped twenty times for you on this trip." Maya shot him an annoyed look.

"Maya. Your brother…"

"Has a nervous bladder. I know. There's always something with him, isn't there?"

That shut me up for once. What was I supposed to say? Yes, there is always something wrong with your brother? Yes, he suffers from anxiety attacks, light autism, strange seizures, occasional loss of bladder control, and maybe some other stuff that the doctors are just waiting to throw at us? Yes, he hasn't been well ever since his dad just took off and only wanted to see him every six months or whenever it suited him? Yes, I could say all those things, but I didn't. What's the point anyway? She knew. Maya knew Victor hadn't been well and she was suffering too, suffering because every hour of my attention went towards him. She was a big girl, now. She was supposed to be able to handle it.

"What's that smell?" she asked, and wrinkled her nose.

"That, my friend, is the smell of Esbjerg," I said and smiled, as I could see the town rise in front of us. "We'll take the boat out to the island from there. It'll be fun once we're on the boat. Just wait and see."

"Yay!" Victor exclaimed. "I love boats."

"It smells like fish," Maya said, and held her nose.

I had to admit, the smell was pretty bad, and opening the window only made it worse. "It's fish," I said, trying to sound cheerful. "Fish guts."

4

1977

It didn't take Astrid many hours to lose track of time, but she guessed it was getting closer to nighttime, since she was beginning to become tired. She decided to lay down a little bit and closed her eyes, and soon she was sound asleep.

It wasn't until the morning that the panic erupted inside of her. She woke up and realized she was still trapped in the bunker and now she was beginning to feel hungry. She got up and walked to the door again. Then she started hammering it.

"Help!" she yelled, but then felt bad. Her mother always told her not to raise her voice.

"You're always so loud, Astrid. And shrill. You should learn to keep your mouth shut. You don't have a pretty voice, and boys like pretty voices, so you stick to what you can do. You cook, alright?"

"Yes, Mom."

Astrid took a deep breath and decided to try again, even if she didn't like to be loud. "HEEELP! I'm in here! I'm trapped! Christian? Can you hear me?"

She stopped and listened for footsteps, or maybe even voices. But still there was nothing. Nothing but the terror of silence.

She tried again. This time she clenched her fists and hammered with all her strength against the iron door, and continued till the pads of her hands became numb. Then she managed to put her fingers into the small crack and tried to rip the door open, but it was stuck.

"Help!" she yelled, while the feeling of utter panic grew.

What if no one hears me? No, you stupid fool. Don't think like that.

She tried to scratch the door with her fingernails, but had to stop because it hurt. Astrid sat down on the step and covered her face with her hands. She was so hungry now. She looked up at the ceiling.

Maybe there was another way out? There had to be an air vent somewhere. Astrid got up and went to the end wall with the shelves. She removed some blankets and touched the wall behind it, felt it, scanned it for anything that could indicate that there was some secret passageway or even a small hole that she could get through.

But there was nothing. She went through the stuff on the shelves meticulously, in the hope that she could find something to use to break the door open. But there was nothing but the flashlight. She rose with it in her hand and ran towards the iron door, swinging and smashing it against the door, but it didn't even make a bump.

She cried as she swung it again and again and destroyed the plastic casing, but it never harmed the door in any way.

Astrid fell to the cold stairs.

You really are no good, are you? She heard her mother's

voice say. *Got yourself into trouble again. I knew you would. He's not going to take care of you. Be a damned fool if he did.*

No, no, Dr. Jansen says I'm okay, remember? I'm good and healthy and strong. My man doesn't care about me being smart or anything. He loves me, he said.

You fool. No one loves a retard. No one, I tell you. No one!

Astrid wiped off her tears in disgust. Why did thinking of her mother always do that to her? Why did it always make her feel so bad about herself? No, there had to be a way, there had to be. Astrid stared at the canned food on the shelves, then sprang up and pulled one down. Luckily it was one of those you could pull open. She didn't even need a can opener. This was good, she thought to herself as she pulled the tab and the sweet smell of ravioli hit her nostrils and tricked her deep hunger even more. This was very good. Astrid searched everywhere and finally found a bunch of plastic spoons. Relieved, she sat down and started eating.

Things always looked better on a full stomach, mother used to say. So as soon as Astrid finished this can, she would find a way to get out of there.

ORDER YOUR COPY TODAY!

19037065R00189

Printed in Great Britain
by Amazon